"How long do you plan to stay in town for this time? Ten minutes?" Lindsay asked.

Obviously she hadn't forgiven him for leaving town after high school. Was she upset that he hadn't said goodbye? Or maybe he was reading too much into her anger. Maybe she just thought she needed to protect his grandmother. "I know I'm not here often, but I do love my grandmother, and I'm here now," Bill said.

"Where were you when she had the flu last winter or when someone tried to break into her house or when she almost gave her credit card number to a phone scammer? I'm the one who helped her then."

She sounded hurt that he was trying to exclude her. "I'm sorry. I just thought you might enjoy a little time off." *Plus, I'm not sure my heart can take being around you every day.*

Books by Missy Tippens

Love Inspired

Her Unlikely Family
His Forever Love

MISSY TIPPENS

Born and raised in Kentucky, Missy met her very own hero when she headed off to grad school in Atlanta, Georgia. She promptly fell in love and hasn't left Georgia since. She and her pastor husband have been married twenty-plus years now, and have been blessed with three wonderful children and an assortment of pets. Nowadays, in addition to her writing, she teaches as an adjunct instructor at a local technical college.

Missy is thankful to God that she's been called to write stories of love and faith. After ten years of pursuing her dream of publishing, she made her first sale of a full-length novel to Steeple Hill Books' Love Inspired line. She still pinches herself to see if it really happened!

Missy would love to hear from readers through her Web site, www.missytippens.com, or by e-mail: missytippens@aol.com. For those with no Internet access, you can reach her c/o Steeple Hill Books, 233 Broadway, Suite 1001, New York, NY 10279.

His Forever Love
Missy Tippens

Steeple
Hill®

Published by Steeple Hill Books™

STEEPLE HILL BOOKS

Steeple
Hill®

Recycling programs
for this product may
not exist in your area.

ISBN-13: 978-0-373-87534-4

HIS FOREVER LOVE

www.SteepleHill.com

Printed in U.S.A.

For I know the plans I have for you, declares the Lord, plans to prosper you and not to harm you, plans to give you hope and a future.

—*Jeremiah* 29:11

To my husband for being my biggest cheerleader and promoter.

To Belinda Peterson for being a trusted, faithful friend and sister in Christ.

And, as always, to God for giving me the stories.

Acknowledgments

Thank you to my church family for supporting me and loving me. And to the Girls' Night Out Gang (you know who you are!) for helping me stay sane.

Thank you to my kids for allowing Mom to work and for not complaining about eating spaghetti over and over…and over.

I'm so thankful for my critique partner and good friend, Belinda Peterson, for generously and, yes, even cheerfully, reading a zillion versions of this manuscript. And for always being willing to room with me at conferences—snoring and all!

A special thanks to Emily Rodmell and all the wonderful people at Steeple Hill Books for their excellence and their commitment to bringing quality inspirational fiction to the shelves.

Chapter One

Time flew backward at warp speed for Bill Wellington when the name Lindsay Jones popped up on his cell phone.

Warm summer evenings studying on the front porch swing. Working together on projects.

Holding hands around The Forever Tree.

But then he hurtled back to the present as he realized there could be only one reason why she would call.

Granny.

He snapped opened his cell phone. "Lindsay, is Granny okay?"

"She's fine. Sorry to scare you."

He had programmed Lindsay's number into his phone when Granny hired her as a caregiver, so he'd assumed the worst. Relief nearly brought him to his knees. He waited for Lindsay to say more, but she remained silent. "Lindsay?"

"I'm sorry. I—" She sighed. "Your granny did take a fall, so I wanted to let you know. She has a mild concussion, and they're going to X-ray her wrist. But the doctor said she'll be fine."

Tension raced across his shoulders and ran up the back of his neck. "How did it happen?"

"She fell off the back porch early this morning while taking out the trash."

Poor Granny. "She's at the hospital now?"

"Yes. They'll probably keep her overnight for observation."

"I'll head down there as soon as I can get a flight."

"Oh, you don't need to do that. I'll stay with her. And Granny Bea didn't even want me to bother you."

She thought he'd be bothered? "No, I want to come check on her. Other than Drake, she's the only family I have."

She sighed again. "Do you need a ride from the airport?"

With all the sighs, it made him wonder what she thought of him. Or did she even think of him at all anymore? "No, thanks. I'll rent a car."

He closed his phone and clutched it in his palm. *Lindsay Jones. Smart, beautiful, kind, funny.* Since he'd avoided all the high school reunions, he hadn't seen her in nearly fifteen years.

A thrill at seeing her surged through him, then immediately plummeted. He hated the thought of heading home to Magnolia, Georgia, for more than a quick weekend. It would mean facing the townspeople he had escaped right after graduation.

It would mean facing Lindsay, as well. The woman he'd been crazy about from the age of ten, with whom he'd fallen in love in high school.

The woman he'd held hands with around The Forever Tree. And had thought he was destined to marry.

Lindsay knew it was all her fault. She was doubting her abilities as a caregiver.

Granny Bea, her eighty-three-year-old employer, had suffered a concussion and a broken wrist. All because Lindsay had tried to do one more favor for her brother. Had tried to squeeze in one last errand.

Now Granny Bea lay in the hospital, her face contorted in pain. Probably wishing she'd never fired the previous *certified* caregiver.

And worse, Lindsay'd had to call...*him*....

Shame on me for thinking the call is worse. What's worse is Granny Bea's injury.

Lindsay tiptoed into the room. "Granny Bea?"

"Oh, Lindsay, dear, I hate that I went and messed up our workday. I guess I scared you to death."

"It's all my fault for being late."

"Oh, pish-posh. I was too lazy to go down the steps and leaned too far off the porch."

"How do you feel?"

"I've felt better." She gave a weak laugh. "My wrist hurts worse than anything."

Lindsay steeled herself to tell Granny Bea the *good* news. "Well, I have a surprise that will perk you up. Bill's coming to check on you."

Bill Wellington, a brilliant physics professor and researcher. Lindsay's *former* friend.

Granny Bea looked distressed. "Oh, Lindsay. He'll miss his classes."

"I had to let him know."

She pressed a palm to her forehead. "You're right, of course. It'll be wonderful to see him. Thank you, dear."

"Just doing my job." She smiled at Granny Bea as she adjusted the blanket.

Lindsay's best friend Donna Rae rushed into the hospital room. "Are you okay, Bea?"

"Oh, hi, Donna Rae. How'd you get word about my silly fall so fast?"

"Gertie down in the E.R. called Vinny's mom. And she called me. Are you okay?"

"I'm fine. I wish you all would quit fussing over me."

Lindsay caught her friend's attention, then nodded toward the hallway. "We'll be back in a minute, Granny Bea."

Once outside the room, Lindsay said, "I contacted Bill. He'll be here ASAP."

Donna Rae's face lit up. "So God's at work."

"What?"

"Oh, never mind." With an impish grin, Donna Rae rubbed her hands together. "Maybe something good will come of the accident. Bill will come to town, and you two will finally be together."

"What on earth are you talking about?"

"The Forever Tree."

Lindsay groaned. The Forever Tree was a huge, old pecan tree that stood proudly in the park downtown. Donna Rae believed in the town legend that a couple that held hands around the tree would be together forever. Well, just because Donna Rae and her husband were blissfully happy didn't mean it worked. After all, Lindsay held Bill's hands around it, and look how that turned out. "Forget the stupid legend. I'm worried about seeing Bill."

"When was the last time you two talked to each other?"

"We haven't. Not since he deserted me."

Donna Rae rolled her eyes. "He didn't desert you. He went off to college."

"And never once called. Never answered my letter. Never visited."

"And you haven't even talked since Bea hired you?"

"There's never been the need. Until now."

"Well, I'm excited. You're destined to be together."

Lindsay leaned back and thunked her head against the wall. Her friend was way off base. "We were never more than friends, but the thought of seeing him again scares me."

Donna Rae gave a deep, throaty laugh.

"Don't laugh at me. I'm nervous. And just you watch. I'll end up with a migraine before it's all over."

"It'll be fine. I'm sure he'll be glad to see you again."

Yeah, right. He'd missed her friendship so much that he'd ignored her for the last fifteen years. They'd been the best of friends. Or so she thought. But two days after graduation, he'd left town. Just disappeared without so much as a goodbye.

Apparently their friendship meant nothing to him. And that still hurt. She would have to steel herself for his arrival.

That evening, Lindsay watched Granny Bea try to grip a fork and scoop a bite of green beans into her mouth with her right wrist enclosed in a spanking-new cast. The cast was brilliant white except for Lindsay's and Donna Rae's signatures scrawled in a circular pattern around the wrist area like a pair of bracelets.

A couple of the beans fell down the front of Granny Bea's hospital gown.

"Here, I'll help you," Lindsay said.

"I might as well learn to do it on my own. I'll have the thing for weeks."

"I can help today. You're sore and tired."

Granny Bea harrumphed, but leaned back against her pillow, relenting. "I hate being laid up. What about the community center?"

"Mr. Kennedy and the others covered for us today. You'll be able to go back to work in a couple of days, looking like one of the kids." She smiled at the woman she took care of who was also her friend and coworker. "I know you'll impress Dylan."

"Yes. I'll have to tell him I fell out of a tree or something a bit exciting."

"Mr. Kennedy will sure want to fuss over you."

"Oh, don't even mention his name or you'll get my ire up."

"He's been crazy about you for two years. You should see him mope when you're not at the center."

Granny Bea shook her casted arm. "That man is too young for me. If he hovers, I'll bop him in the head with this thing."

"Granny Bea has a boyfriend," Lindsay sang.

"I may have to test it out on your head first."

Lindsay laughed, then scooped up a bite of beans, held it out to Granny Bea, and watched as she ate it.

A man cleared his throat in the doorway, then rapped on the door. "Granny?"

She'd know that voice anywhere. Had she really thought she could prepare for this moment?

She was afraid to turn around. Afraid of the hurt that might still show on her face even after so many years.

"Bill, honey, you're here!" Granny Bea called. "Come in."

Lindsay pasted a half-smile on her face, then swiveled around to see him.

Oh, my. She couldn't believe what she was seeing. She absolutely could not believe this was Bill Wellington. Tall, skinny, nerdy, bookworm Bill had been transformed during his years away.

Tall. Yes, he was still tall. But that's where the similarities ended. He had filled out. And had turned into an attractive man. How could that have happened?

He hurried to his granny's side, then hugged her. "How are you feeling?" He was so careful, so concerned, that it gave Lindsay's heartstrings a big, ol' yank.

"I'm fine, son."

He looked up from Granny Bea and smiled in Lindsay's direction. "Hi, Lindsay."

After several seconds of staring at this near stranger, she realized she hadn't acknowledged his greeting. "Oh, hi. Good to see you again. Wow. You're all grown-up." *Way to go, Lindsay. Stating the obvious.*

"Yes, fifteen years have a way of doing that. But you look exactly the same. I would have recognized you anywhere."

And she couldn't have picked him out of a police lineup if her life depended on it. His dark brown, shaggy hair was now short and layered and looked as if it had lightened in the sun. His gaunt, pale face was now tanned, angular, masculine. And his beanpole body was now muscle-bound.

"Broken wrist, huh?" He touched Granny Bea's cast. Then he craned his neck, trying to read the signatures. Once he completed reading the circle of permanent marker, he smiled at Lindsay.

Her traitorous heart galloped underneath her rib cage. *Stop it! I will not let my heart race over this man. This supposed friend.*

"Lindsay, I appreciate you bringing her to the hospital. I'm sure you're worn out. I'll stay with her tonight."

She bristled. He'd marched in and was going to try to take over Granny Bea's care.

He's her grandson. He has every right to.

Still, it made her mad that he lived his life way up there in Boston and barely ever spent time with his granny.

"I can stay," she said. "I imagine you're tired from traveling."

"I dozed a little on the flight. Go on home. I'll call you if she needs anything."

"He's right, dear. You've been here all day."

What could she do? "Okay. I'll come back tomorrow morning with some fresh clothes for her."

"Thanks." He started to hold out a hand, as if he were going to shake her hand, but then the gesture ended up as a little wave. A somewhat dorky wave, more like the Bill she remembered.

She was comforted by the fact that he was still Bill. Yet that little wave reminded her of the friend she'd lost.

Bill wasn't sure he'd be able to catch his breath until Lindsay was gone. He had to get a grip or she might think she needed to rush him down to the E.R.

Her eyes were still as violet-blue, her hair as deep red, thick and smooth as it had been when she was eighteen.

He was a complete sap. A thirty-three-year-old acting like a lovesick teenager.

He walked to the other side of Granny's bed, putting distance between him and Lindsay. *She's only a woman like any other. Nothing special. Just happens to have been blessed with gorgeous eyes and hair. And just happens to be the girl I fell in love with ages ago.*

"Well, Granny Bea, I'll see you bright and early." Lindsay kissed Granny's head. "Make Bill take good care of you."

"Thanks for everything, dear. Get some rest, and we'll see you tomorrow."

Lindsay smiled fondly at Granny, which didn't help his composure a bit. She stepped toward the door. "Good night." She made brief eye contact with Bill, but then turned and left.

"So you fell off the porch while taking out the trash?" he asked.

She huffed. "Yes. Silly on my part."

"I thought you hired Lindsay to help with that."

"I did. But she was running late this morning—had to get the boys at the last minute."

"The boys?"

"Her nephews. Her brother Gregory is divorced and has sole custody. Lindsay's like a mother to his boys and keeps them a good bit. She was about to take them to day care this morning, then she and I were going to go to work."

"Work?"

"At the community center. They hired her as director, and I'm working as her assistant."

"You mean you're volunteering?"

"At first I was. Now I'm hired." She grinned, and looked so proud. "My first job outside the home—at age eighty-three."

His granny working? But her home was her life. She'd always been there for him and his brother Drake after his parents died, moving them in with her—cooking, cleaning, helping with homework, chauffeuring them to lessons and Drake to sports practices.

"Why would you get a job now? You don't need the money."

"That's a silly question. I love it! It gives me a reason to get out of bed each day."

Had Granny been depressed? Had she been lonely? "You won't be able to work with that cast."

"Oh, I don't think this'll stop me."

"Well, I want to talk with the doctor tomorrow. There's always the concussion to consider."

She waved away his concerns. "You should go to the house for the night, son. Don't try to sleep here."

He looked around the room and spotted a chair. "I bet that folds out into a recliner. I'll be fine here."

She smiled at him, and her lower lip quivered. "I'm so happy to see you, baby. It's nice to have you home. Even if I had to break my arm to get you here." She patted his cheek. "I'm teasing."

It was the truth, though. He'd been away for too long. And whenever he did visit, it was a brief thirty-six-hour stay. He usually flew in on a Friday night, spent Saturday at Granny's, maybe took her out to eat in Athens, then flew out early Sunday morning. He tried to avoid the townspeople. He had never fit in here.

Maybe he should hang around for a couple of days. To make sure she would be okay with her right arm out of commission. But if she could fall off her own porch doing something as simple as carrying out the trash, he suspected she might be getting too feeble to live alone. "I'm glad to be home. I'd like to stay until I make sure you're okay on your own."

"Oh, good. We'll break out of this joint tomorrow and have a nice time together. You, me and Lindsay."

Lindsay? Why would she say that? Sure, they worked together some. But Granny wouldn't need her while he was there.

A nurse stuck her head in the door as she knocked. "Mrs. Wellington, how about getting up before my shift's over? I imagine you're ready to go to sleep for a little while." She looked at Bill. "And if you're staying, we'll get your chair fixed up with a blanket and pillow."

"Thanks."

As the nurse helped Granny out of bed, Bill excused himself to wait in the hallway. But before he left, he noticed what a hard time they had getting Granny out of bed, then how slowly she moved. She'd definitely aged a lot since the last time he'd been home. And a broken wrist would make getting around even harder.

He had to wonder how much longer she'd be able to live on her own. He would watch her closely the next few days.

You, me and Lindsay.

Chapter Two

Bill helped Granny in the front door of her house. She seemed worn out from the short trip home from the hospital, and leaned heavily on his arm.

"Help me into my chair. I think I'll rest a bit."

The sight of her recliner caused a pang in his gut. So many memories of sitting with her in that chair, her rocking him when he was young, then sharing the chair side-by-side, squeezed in together, when he thought he was too old for rocking.

He closed his eyes and let the familiar smells wash over him. *Home.* At least it was home as far as he could remember. Though he had memories of his mom and dad, they had always traveled extensively, so Granny had been the stability in his life.

Lindsay, who'd insisted on following them home, slipped in the front door, put a blanket over Granny's lap, then pulled a TV tray in front of her. Once she'd turned on the television, she put the remote on the table. "Here you go. Have a nice nap."

He motioned to her to join him in the kitchen. "You know, Lindsay, while I'm here, Granny won't really need your help."

"And how long do you plan to stay this time? Ten minutes?"

Obviously, she hadn't forgiven him for leaving town after high school. Or maybe he was reading too much into her anger.

Maybe she just thought she needed to protect Granny. "I know I'm not here often, but I do love my grandmother."

"Where were you when she had the flu last winter or when someone tried to break into her house one night? I'm the one who helped her then. And I'm the one who was here to keep her from giving out her credit card number in a phone scam."

She sounded hurt that he had tried to exclude her. "I'm sorry. I just thought you might enjoy a little time off." *Plus, I'm not sure I can be around you every day.*

She slumped into a chair at the table. "No. I'm sorry for jumping down your throat. I'm worried about her and don't want to be shut out while she's recovering."

"That's fine. I'm sure I can use your help."

"Thank you." She stood and reached for the back door. "Well, I guess I need to go check out back. I think we left a mess of trash after her fall."

While Lindsay was outside, the seriousness of Granny's situation hit Bill. She'd been ill with the flu. And had had someone try to break in and someone else try to rip her off. She was old and vulnerable. Probably needed someone with her around the clock.

Maybe the fall would turn out to be for the good. It helped him face what he'd always known—at some point he and Granny would reverse roles, and he would become the caregiver.

The time had come for him to move Granny to live with him.

He took a deep breath. When he blew it out, he felt lighter, happier. It would be nice to have Granny nearby. Nice to have a family.

When Lindsay came in from tidying up the backyard, Bill blindsided her with the most ridiculous request. "Are you crazy?" she asked.

He stepped back as if she'd breathed fire on him. If only she could.

"I'm simply asking for your help," he said.

"No. There's your answer. I won't help you tell your poor granny that she has to quit her new job, sell her beloved home, leave all her lifelong friends, and move up where it snows all the time."

"It doesn't snow all the time."

Of course. Mr. Brain missed the point entirely. "Your grandmother does fine on her own. Whatever feebleness you thought you saw was due to her fall. She's probably bruised, sore. And for your information, the flu and scam artists hang out in Boston, too."

"So I'm assuming I can't count on you to help me break the news?"

She gave him a look that said *get a clue.*

He turned and went toward the living room. Lindsay wanted to escape. She couldn't stand having to witness what he was about to do. But maybe she and Granny could change his mind.

She followed him, but paused before entering, listening.

Bill mumbled soft words she couldn't decipher.

Granny laughed. Cackled, actually. "I'm not getting feeble, son. I just took a fall. And look, I didn't break. Well, except for the wrist."

As Lindsay walked in, Bill said, "You're getting to an age where you may need some help."

"Lindsay gives me all the help I need. Which is mainly a ride around town. I'm not driving much anymore."

Lindsay took her place beside Granny Bea. "She's insisted on keeping her license and car, but I don't let her drive. So don't worry about that."

"It's for an emergency," Granny Bea added.

Bill looked from Granny Bea to her, then back. "I've been thinking about this move off and on for a few years. At one time, I even checked out an adult day-care facility near my office. You would have activities during the day, then I would be home with you at night."

"I have plenty of activities here. Lindsay and I coordinate trips for the seniors' group at church. And we work three days a week at the community center—all those precious, needy kids, plus a few old codgers who are lonely and come to volunteer. They keep me young. I couldn't give that up."

"Well, looks like that's two votes against one." Lindsay held up two fingers on one hand and one finger on the other. "I guess Granny Bea will be staying here."

Apparently, Bill didn't appreciate her scorekeeping. He didn't crack a smile, and she could practically see the cogs working in his mind.

He could think all he wanted. She wasn't budging.

As Granny began to nod off, Bill walked through the house, noting the condition of each room. Carpet needed replacing. When they'd driven up, he'd noticed the roof was on its last leg.

They had a good bit of work ahead of them if they were going to sell the house. Not to mention the accumulation of belongings from over fifty years in the house.

Lindsay followed him through the rooms, watching his every move. "What are you doing?" she finally asked.

"I'm certain Granny will come around to the idea of moving in with me. I'm noting repairs that need to be done before putting the house on the market."

"Your grandmother is fine. Give her time to recover before you make any drastic decisions."

"It's not just the fall. She's vulnerable here all alone."

"Just promise me you won't make a knee-jerk decision."

"I never do that."

She nodded. She knew he took a scientific approach to life. At least he used to. "Well, I guess I'll go throw something together for dinner."

"You don't have to do that. I can take over from here."

"Cooking her meals is part of my job."

Three times he'd hired someone to help Granny, and she'd fired every one of them. And now she'd hired Lindsay herself. "Okay. Well, let me know if you need any help."

She eyed him warily. "You can cook?"

He smiled. "According to my coworkers, I'm a great cook. Granny taught me."

"Hmm. I'll holler if I need you." She headed toward the kitchen with one quick glance over her shoulder. As if she didn't trust him.

It was no wonder she didn't trust him. Cooking. Or otherwise. He'd left town fifteen years ago without any warning.

But he'd been crazy about her. He'd been her lab partner and study partner for years, while silently wishing for more. Then during their senior year, despite the fact that she was dating Joey Peck, he'd decided it was time to tell her how he felt about her.

He'd resisted all along because he was such a joke at school. He was sure she wouldn't even consider dating the school's number-one geek. But as graduation approached, he sensed a new relationship forming. She seemed more confident, more sure of who she was and where she was going.

And maybe it had been wishful thinking, but he thought he'd detected a flash of attraction one night while they studied for finals side by side on Granny's porch swing.

So he'd gone out and bought her an angel figurine for her collection. It had a plaque that said I Love You. His hands had shaken as he paid for it, then wrapped it up. He'd sent Granny and his brother to the movie that night, and invited Lindsay over. He waited in the swing with the wrapped gift.

She'd shown up squealing, flashing a microscopic diamond on her left ring finger. The thing seemed to wink at him when the stone caught the rays of the setting sun and flashed with each movement as she snatched up the gift, then tore off the wrapping paper.

When she first saw the angel, she froze in place.

He'd sat silently. In shock. Grieving. Mortified.

Then she'd smiled at him, but he could see the question in her eyes.

Because he couldn't stand for her to know the truth, he told her she was the best friend a guy could ever have.

She'd shown relief, then had chatted about the wedding plans over dinner.

It was the longest night of his life.

The next day he loaded his car to the roof and informed Granny he was going to move to Boston early. He left and never looked back. He couldn't bear to do otherwise.

He shook his head and himself back to the present. No, Lindsay probably shouldn't trust him. He'd told her she was important to him then abandoned her. He'd taken the cowardly way out when he'd left town. And he'd felt terrible about not answering her phone call and letter. But he'd gone into self-protect mode. He'd had to.

Now he was back in Magnolia and had already upset her. No wonder she looked at him askance.

Once he'd unpacked, Bill found Granny snoozing in her chair in front of the blaring TV. He turned the volume down, and as he did so, she stirred.

"Wh—what's wrong?" she asked groggily.

He couldn't help but laugh. She'd slept through the cacophony of the evening news, but woke when the room got quiet.

"It's me, Granny."

"Oh, Bill, honey, I'm so glad you're still here." She lurched forward a couple of times trying to stand, but couldn't get out of her chair. He took her arm and helped pull her up, then hugged her, relishing the familiar fragrance of her hair and her face powder.

He held her away from him to get a good look. "How are your head and arm feeling?"

"Both fine. No pain at all."

"Good. Lindsay's making dinner. Are you hungry?"

"Starving."

"So, how many days a week does she come?"

"She stays with me on Tuesdays and Thursdays, the days we're not working at the community center. Plus, she's always checked on me on the weekends anyway."

"I'm glad you've had someone to take care of you. But I think we really do need to talk about moving you to Boston."

She looked around the room and appeared to retreat to her own world. A smile lit her face. "I won't ever be ready to leave this place, son, even though I do realize sometimes we have to do things we don't want to do. Of course, it's not time yet. I'll let you know when it is."

"I'm sorry, Granny. With the fall and all, and the fact that you've already needed Lindsay's help, I think it may be time now."

With eyebrows drawn together, she tilted her head back to look him in the eye. "Could you ever see yourself moving here to live?"

He'd like to spare her feelings, but had to be honest. "No. I'm sorry."

"Don't be sorry. You have your life, and I wouldn't try to drag you back here if you didn't want it."

"You know it's not that I wouldn't want to be with you."

"I know, dear. But I hate that you never felt at home in Magnolia."

Granny had tried so hard to make them happy, but neither he nor Drake had ever adjusted very well after they'd come to live with her. "Yeah. I'm sorry."

"Excuse me," Lindsay said from the doorway. "Dinner is ready."

"We'll be right there, dear. Can you stay?"

"I can't today." She looked at Bill. "I usually cook for my dad and brother's family."

"Gregory?"

"Yes. He and his two children live across the street from Dad."

"What about Richard?" Bill suspected Lindsay's other brother no longer lived in Magnolia.

"He manages a hotel in Atlanta."

"I'm sorry to hear about Gregory's divorce."

She snapped a dish towel and folded it somewhat violently.

"It was a bad scene. She deserted them all. For a rich lawyer in Atlanta."

"That girl was trouble from the start," Granny said.

"What she did to those babies is criminal," Lindsay said, her face red in anger. "I'll go put the bread in the oven." She left the room quickly.

Granny sighed. "Lindsay suffered terrible migraines through the whole ordeal. But Hunter and Chase have suffered the most. Not to mention poor Gregory."

"Maybe he'll find the right woman next time." But how could he be sure? How could anyone be sure? "Shall we go eat?" he asked Granny, holding out his arm for her.

"I'd love to, kind sir." She winked at him, and his heart swelled. It would be so nice to have her live with him. He'd missed her.

As Granny Bea and Bill walked into the kitchen, Lindsay flinched, thinking he would hit his head on the door frame. Luckily, the older house had taller ceilings. And it seemed he ducked out of habit even if he didn't need to.

"How tall are you now, anyway?" she asked before she thought about it.

"Six-foot-six-and-a-half."

"You weren't that tall in high school."

"No. I grew a few inches in college, and put on about fifty pounds over the years."

She didn't doubt it. He had been way too skinny in high school. And now he was…well…just right.

Refusing to think about how handsome he was, she set about putting the food on the table. "Y'all have a seat."

"May I help?" he offered.

"No, it's all ready." In her experience, anytime a man tried to help in the kitchen, it ended in disaster.

Once she had everything on the table, Granny Bea reached for her hand. "Stay for a few minutes, dear. Sit and talk with us."

She never could turn Granny Bea down. "Okay. For a

minute." Before she could sit in the chair next to Granny Bea, Bill jumped up and pulled it out for her.

She hesitated, then laughed. "Sorry. Growing up with two brothers makes me a little nervous when my chair is pulled out for me."

He nodded. "Ah, the old yank-the-chair-out-from-under-you trick. I had that happen to me in school many times."

She was sorry she had brought it up when she noticed the haunted look on his face. Kids in Magnolia had been awful to him.

He nicely pushed her chair in for her. "Thank you." A small, gentlemanly gesture, but very nice for a woman who never had time for dating anymore.

"Can you ladies help me make a list of the repairs that need to be made around here? When I came in, I noticed the roof is in bad shape."

Lindsay knew his interest wasn't because he cared about the condition of the house. He was already moving on with his plan to sell it. "Nothing's urgent. Maybe you can get the roof done on this visit and save the rest for another time."

"The carpet in the bedrooms is shot," Granny Bea said. "I've even had Lindsay take me to look at some samples, but couldn't decide what to do."

Granny Bea didn't get it. She thought he was interested in helping her. Helping move her out the door was more like it.

Bill looked from one of them to the other. "We'll have to get right on it. I'll make some calls tomorrow."

"He's going to be here a few days, Lindsay," Granny Bea said, then patted his hand. "You did say you can stay a few days, Bill?"

"Yes. But I need to check in with my office first."

So they had a few days to change his mind. Once he saw Granny get back to normal, he would have to back down.

Lindsay ran her fingernail in a groove scratched into the table's finish. "So, *Dr. Wellington.* I hear you're teaching physics at the university. Very impressive."

He waved off the compliment as if embarrassed. "Not nearly as glamorous as it sounds."

"And doing research, too?"

"Yes, particle physics. We've been doing neutrino oscillation studies, and we've also begun work trying to come up with ways to detect dark matter. In fact, I've applied for a grant. I hope to hear something soon."

"Good luck on the grant. Sounds interesting."

"Yes, it's—" His golden-brown eyes sparkled. "Never mind. I would tell you more, but you would probably want to go jump off a bridge. I have that effect on people."

She smiled at his self-deprecating humor. The guy was truly sweet. She'd managed to forget that fact over the years. Her stomach fluttered, and she couldn't pull her gaze away from his. She wanted to ask him what physical principle made him so hypnotic.

She jumped up from the table. "I would love to hear more later. But it's time to pick up the boys." She turned to Granny Bea. "I'll stop by to see how you're feeling in the morning." She waved as she hurried out.

She and Granny needed a plan. And they needed it fast. Tomorrow morning, they could put their heads together and strategize. With the two of them together, Bill wouldn't stand a chance.

The next morning, Lindsay rushed to move herself and her nephews out the door of Gregory's house so she could stop at Granny Bea's on the way to the center. Normally unflappable Lindsay was totally flapped. The boys always did that to her. At least until she got to the breaking point. Then the boys seemed to sense they were on her very last nerve and would back down.

She was within an inch of that point.

She jammed her hands on her hips. "If you don't behave, I won't take you to the movie this weekend."

They continued to chase each other around the coffee table, but glanced her way as if testing the waters. They were nervous.

"One. Two…"

They darted to opposite ends of the couch to find their shoes.

"Two and a half…"

"I'm weady!" Chase jumped up with his shoes on the wrong feet. "I beat Hunter. I win!"

"No you didn't. You got 'em backwards." Hunter smirked at his little brother. "So I win."

"…Three. Grab your book bags and head out the door right now." Lindsay pointed.

They weren't bad boys. They just needed a little firmness for a change. Her poor brother still couldn't get a handle on that fact. He was trying to make up for their mother deserting them. At four and five years old, all they knew was that they wanted someone to love them. Gregory loved them like crazy, but sometimes didn't know how to show it. He owned his own business and worked all the time to provide for his family.

She grabbed her purse and locked the door behind them. "Okay. March. To the car. I'll drop you at day care and your daddy will pick you up." She glanced at her watch. "I'll barely make it to Granny Bea's on time."

"I hate day care. Ith for babies," Chase said with his chubby four-year-old cheeks causing a slight lisp.

"You *are* a baby. So shut up," his brother said.

As Lindsay buckled them into their booster seats, she pointed at Hunter. "We don't say 'shut up' in this family. And if you aren't nice to each other—"

"You won't take us to the movie," Hunter finished for her. "We know."

The little sweethearts folded their hands in their laps and settled.

When they arrived at the Jolly-time Day Care Center, she hurried them inside and gave them a quick kiss.

Chase grabbed tightly around her neck and wouldn't let go. "I wuv you, Aunt Windsay."

She hugged him back, enjoying the smell of baby shampoo and little boy. "I love you, too, baby." He wiggled out of her clutches and ran off.

A pang of regret gave her heart a squeeze. Though she was

usually content in her singlehood, there were times when she wished more than anything that she had a husband and kids of her own. But apparently, that wasn't in God's plan.

She was fine on her own, though. Plus, the boys needed her.

When she arrived at Granny Bea's house, she was relieved to find her sitting on the front porch swing. Time for a quick private talk.

"Good morning, Granny Bea."

"Mornin', dear. Have a seat and swing a bit."

"We need to form a plan," she whispered as she dropped into the swing, then looked around for evidence of Bill's presence.

"He's in the kitchen cooking breakfast," Granny Bea whispered back. "Why are we talking so quietly?"

"So he won't hear us figuring out how to get him to let you stay here."

"Aha. Well, I think I can get him to cooperate. Or else I'll turn him over my knee." She laughed.

Granny Bea didn't understand how serious Bill was. "He seems determined, so we have to fight. Plan A is we show him how involved you are at the community center."

"I think you're right. And we also show him how well you and I do together."

Lindsay sat up straighter, excited that this might actually work. "Yeah. We're a team. Then maybe he won't worry that you're alone."

"I'll drag him to every activity at the center so he'll see how important my position is."

Lindsay nodded. "See if you can manage coming in for a while today, if you feel up to it."

"I feel perfectly fine. And the doctor didn't say I had to limit my activity."

"Okay. We have a plan." She held out her hand to Granny Bea to shake on it. With the cast, they had to shake fingers.

Bill walked outside as they did so. "What's going on?"

"I just dropped by to check on Granny Bea." Lindsay hopped up. "I'm heading to the center now."

"How about some biscuits and bacon first?"

Mmm. Biscuits were her favorite, and she hadn't had time to eat while feeding Hunter and Chase. "Thanks, but I don't have time."

"They're world-famous biscuits. Well, Boston-famous anyway."

Lindsay raised an eyebrow.

"Campus-famous? I'm serious, though. They're the best, even if I do say so myself."

"Maybe another time." She waved as she walked toward her car, her stomach growling.

Bill probably had the mistaken notion that Granny Bea sat around her house all the time waiting for his visits, that she had no life of her own beyond him and Drake. He pictured her wasting away on her own—lonely, decrepit. Maybe if he saw evidence of Granny's vitality, he would get beyond his limited imaginings.

Maybe if Mr. Kennedy pursued Granny Bea more than ever, Bill would realize she had a life of her own. Besides, Mr. Kennedy was only seventy-four years old. A *youngster* who could take care of her if she ever needed help.

Lindsay practically rubbed her hands together in delight. She would speak to Granny Bea's suitor as soon as he arrived to volunteer that day. And he *would* be there. He hadn't missed a day since Granny Bea began working.

"Bill, honey, I need a ride to work today."

His grandmother hadn't been home from the hospital for a full twenty-four hours. "You should be recovering, Granny."

"My doctor didn't place any limitations on me, and other than the bother of the cast, I feel perfectly normal."

What could he do? Perhaps call on her maternal instincts? "How about staying home to visit with me today?"

"You're right. I don't want to miss the chance to visit with you. So you're coming with me." She grabbed her purse and headed out the front door. "Come on, son. I'm already late."

So much for spending the morning making phone calls about the house. He patted his pocket to make sure he had his cell phone. He could make calls from the community center.

As they drove toward the town square, he caught Granny staring at him. "What?"

"It's so nice to have you here. I'm tickled that everyone at the center will get to meet you. You'll be a good role model for the little ones."

"I still can't believe you're working there. How old are the kids?"

"Age three and up."

"Do Gregory's boys come?"

"No, they're in full-time day care. The three- and four-year-olds only come in the mornings. In the afternoons, we have the after-school children. And senior citizens from the church come in the morning to socialize and to serve as volunteers to help with the children."

He couldn't believe his Granny hadn't mentioned this. "Did you get started with the church group?"

"I'm actually the one who started the senior volunteer program. And I've applied for a grant to help fund a lunch program for the preschoolers."

As he pulled into a parking place, he gaped at his grandmother. "You're kidding."

"Maybe I should be offended," she said with a smile.

"I'm sorry. I didn't mean it that way. I'm truly impressed."

"Maybe we'll both receive our grants." She patted his cheek. "Now come help me out of the car."

He hurried around to open her door and give her a hand. Then she led the way inside. This new Granny was such a surprise. A nice surprise. Maybe he had Lindsay to thank for Granny's newfound happiness and fulfillment.

As soon as they walked in, a dapperly dressed elderly gentleman hurried over to them. "Bea! Oh, Bea, are you okay? I heard you broke your wrist." His face flamed red all the way to the top of his balding head.

She shooed at him as if he were a bothersome fly. "I'm perfectly fine, Mr. Kennedy." Then she brushed past him.

Bill choked back a chuckle. The poor guy. Reminded him of how he felt his freshman year of high school whenever he had tried to make conversation with Lindsay. He'd followed her around like a lost puppy dog waiting for her to notice him, and when she had, he'd invariably made dumb, nonsensical comments.

The woman herself was leaning over a child at a small table, pointing to something the child was drawing with a crayon. Her deep red hair that used to hang all the way down her back now swung just below her chin, curving toward her face. She pushed it behind her ear as she smiled at the child.

He inhaled deeply to try to catch his breath. How could she still affect him so? Maybe he and Mr. Kennedy had a bit more in common than he first thought.

He turned to the man, who seemed engrossed in Granny's every move. "Hi, Mr. Kennedy. I'm Bill Wellington, Bea's grandson."

"Oh, Bea talks about you all the time. You and your brother. I'm glad to finally meet you."

"She insisted on working today, even after being in the hospital yesterday."

"Stubborn woman. Believe me, I know."

Bill swiped his hand over his mouth to keep from laughing at the frustration in the man's voice. Then a sobering thought hit him. He would be taking Granny away from a man who obviously had a crush on her.

At least Granny didn't seem to care for Mr. Kennedy.

"Bill, come meet the children," Granny called from a low table across the room.

She introduced him to each child sitting around the table. One little boy seemed especially attached to Granny. He clung to her leg as she handed out papers.

"And this is Dylan. He's my helper today."

"I got to sign her cast," Dylan told him proudly.

"Oh, let me see." Bill checked out his scribbled name in purple marker. "Nice job."

Granny ruffled the boy's hair. "Dylan, why don't you sit down and work the puzzle with the rest of the children."

"Okay, Granny Bea." He slid into a small wooden chair and began to connect the dots on the page. His tongue hung out of the corner of his mouth as he concentrated.

Granny beamed at Bill. "This is what I look forward to three days a week."

Lindsay approached. "Granny Bea, now that the kids are busy, could you go ahead and start the bingo game for our adults?"

"Sure thing. Be back in a jiffy." She hurried to the other side of the room, full of more energy than ever before.

"How long do the little ones stay?" he asked Lindsay.

"We feed them lunch, peanut butter and jelly sandwiches donated from our church right now. But your grandmother has applied for a federal grant for funding for a fuller meal."

"She mentioned that. When do the older kids get here?"

"After school, around three o'clock. We feed them a snack, help with homework, then play educational games."

"And the center is open three days a week?"

She reached over to pick up a crayon Dylan had dropped, then patted him on the back. "So far. We hope to move to five days a week in the next year or so. It was a small program we started as a ministry at the church one day a week, but we're working with the county to get it fully funded. They're already providing the building."

"Impressive."

"Your granny has had a lot to do with the success of the program. We really need her." She stared at him as if in challenge. She appeared very determined.

So was he. "I understand."

Granny walked up. "So, Bill, what do you think of our little community center?"

"It's amazing what you've all done. Kudos to both of you."

"Bea?" Mr. Kennedy tapped her on the shoulder.

She huffed as if irritated. "Yes?"

"Would you go out to dinner with me this evening?"

Granny slapped a hand to her chest. "Why, Mr. Kennedy, you can't fraternize with the staff."

"I didn't ask you to *fraternize*. I only asked you to dinner."

Obviously flustered, she sputtered, "I can't do anything tonight. I have company."

"Well, that's the problem. I hear Bill may be moving you up to Boston, and I can't bear to see you go." He tugged on his bow tie, which left it slightly crooked.

Bill arched his brows at Lindsay. Seemed she'd been talking to Granny's...not-quite-boyfriend.

"That's none of your concern, sir." Granny marched away and sat on a small chair at the table with the children.

A dejected Mr. Kennedy left the center.

"Nice try, Lindsay."

"What do you mean?"

"If moving Granny to Boston is best for her, then that's what I need to do. You can't try to sway my decision by manipulating a poor old man who has a crush on her."

She made no comment, but her face reddened. With her creamy, clear complexion, even the slightest blush had always sent streaks of red along her cheeks and down her neck. If the embarrassment or nervousness continued, she'd end up with hives on her neck and chest.

Never mind her scheming. He had work to do. "I'm going back to Granny's to make some calls. You know, if Granny's well enough to work, then she won't need you helping her as much while I'm here. Why don't you take tomorrow off?"

"I don't mind coming—we have our routine, you know."

"Enjoy a paid day off. Granny and I could use some time together."

She frowned. "But she doesn't pay me for weekends. I like to visit."

That made it a little more difficult to keep her away. And

truly, it wasn't as if he didn't want her around. He just didn't want her meddling. "No, I insist you take a break from the extra responsibility. Rest. Get caught up at home."

"Okay. I can take a hint."

His own face burned, probably as red as hers. "What time this afternoon should I come back to pick up Granny?"

"I can bring her home when we leave at six."

"She works the whole day?"

"It's only three days a week. And she gets a break between one and three o'clock."

"Does she go home to rest?"

"No, she usually hangs out here with me."

"Helping you work?"

"You know, you should probably talk to your grandmother about her work schedule. I need to get back to the kids." She walked away in a huff.

Of course, he had been somewhat accusatory. But he needed to make sure Lindsay wasn't overworking Granny.

Past experience told him Lindsay wouldn't do that. But he couldn't let ancient memories sway decisions he needed to make in the present.

Chapter Three

The next morning, Lindsay reflected on how she had nearly messed up by pushing Mr. Kennedy on Granny Bea. The poor man hadn't felt comfortable asking Bea out yet, so Lindsay had pretty much begged him to. Now Bill was on to them. She'd have to be more subtle.

So, she would do what Bill had insisted she do. She would stay away. Only for today, though.

She cleaned an already clean house. Washed two small loads of laundry. Ate frozen waffles heated in the toaster. Sipped a cup of coffee. Read the newspaper and clipped coupons. Watered the front-porch flowerpots full of begonias and impatiens. Swept dirt off the sidewalk.

And the clock on the mantel said ten o'clock.

A.m.

How would she spend a whole day without visiting Granny Bea or without taking care of Hunter and Chase? There weren't any activities at church that day. Her dad was working in his yard.

Maybe she could visit Donna Rae. See if she could help her around the house for a while. She must have a ton of work to do with that houseful of kids.

She pulled a pound cake out of the freezer to take to them.

She always made two so she'd have an extra on hand to give away. Today seemed like a good occasion.

When she arrived, Vinny's car was gone. But he usually showed houses on Saturday, so she wasn't surprised.

She walked in the front door without knocking. They hadn't knocked on each other's doors for twenty years, if ever. "Hello."

"In here," Donna Rae called from the kitchen. She was elbow-deep in dishwashing suds. "Oh, hey, Lindsay. What brings you by?"

"I come bearing sweets." She set the cake on the counter.

"Oh, I hope it's a chocolate pound cake."

"Not chocolate. Sour cream."

"Yummy. I've been craving chocolate, though." She bit her lip and wouldn't look at Lindsay.

No way. "You're kidding, aren't you? A late April Fools' Day joke?"

"April Fools' was a month ago."

"So you're not kidding. You're pregnant? *Again?*"

She smiled a radiant smile. "Yes, number five, and I'm thrilled. So don't look so shocked and disappointed."

She held up her hands in surrender. "Hey, I'm happy if you're happy. That's all that matters." She hugged her friend and tried to be genuinely happy. But sometimes she battled the green-eyed monster.

"Don't tell anyone yet. We want to wait a few more weeks, then tell our family."

"Okay. Are you sick yet?"

"No. And maybe, God willing, I won't be this time."

Lindsay practically snorted. "Yeah, right."

"On to better subjects. Has Bill asked you out yet?"

She did snort a laugh that time. "Are you kidding? He arrived, spent about five minutes with Granny Bea, then decided that she needs to move up there to live with him."

"Well, you've always said he needs to be thinking more about taking care of her."

"I meant for him to move home to do so."

"Can you blame the guy? He has this illustrious career up there. Why would he move back to Magnolia?"

"You have a point. I guess he'll have to trust us to watch over her."

Donna Rae looked away as she slowly dried her hands on a dish towel. "You could help him take care of her. Up there in Boston—one of the places you've always wanted to visit, if you recall."

"Don't tell me you have pregnancy mush-brain already. This is a record. It's hitting in the first trimester."

Donna Rae turned and grabbed Lindsay's hands, serious all of a sudden. "I have a feeling about this. I've always had a strong sense that you two were meant for each other."

Scary, because whenever Donna Rae had strong "senses," she was almost always right. Maybe it came from being such a prayer warrior—always in close contact with God. "Why didn't you ever mention it before?"

"I didn't want to say anything before it was God's timing for you two. But ever since you said his name yesterday, I've had chills up my back when I think of it."

"Well, stop it. Your ideas about The Forever Tree and this chill-bump thing, they're worrying me. Because there's no way I could ever move up there. I can't leave Chase and Hunter. They need me."

Donna Rae sighed, then shook her head. "I know. I guess God will figure it all out if it's in His plan."

Plan, my foot. The only important plan at the moment was the one that would keep Granny Bea in Magnolia. "Come on. Let's go find something to do."

Donna Rae cackled. "*Find* something to do?" She snatched a piece of paper from under a magnet on her refrigerator door. "Here's my 'Honey Do List.' Go for it."

Lindsay took the mile-long list and decided to number the items to prioritize them. When she finished, number one on the list was *fix the dripping showerhead in kids' bathroom.* She'd done that at her own house, so she headed outside to Vinny's workshop to see if he had the right tools. As she tromped back through the kitchen toward the stairs, Donna Rae hollered, "Thanks, *honey!*"

Cute. Real cute. But at least she had something to occupy her for a few hours.

Bill wanted to throttle Granny. He was beginning to think he'd been totally mistaken. The woman was obviously capable of ordering him around as she went about her daily housework. Maybe she was okay on her own after all.

He glanced at the hastily scrawled directions Granny had given him. He pulled into Donna Rae's driveway, and Lindsay sat on the front steps, looking perturbed. She didn't seem any happier once she climbed in his car.

"I'm sorry Granny interrupted what you were doing."

"It's okay. I was only helping Donna Rae around the house—doing a little plumbing work. The next item on the list was dusting the ceiling fans, so I guess I should thank you."

He tried not to smile at the vision of her under a sink with a wrench. "Granny was insistent that you help me pick out the carpet. I guess she doesn't trust my judgment."

"We've looked at samples before, so she knows I have an idea of what she likes."

"I called and tried to arrange a day for Arnie's Carpets to come. They weren't very helpful. Didn't have anything open until two weeks out. As it is, I'm afraid I'll be here a week."

He thought Lindsay grinned, but then she turned toward the car window as she spoke. "I imagine Molly made the appointment. She might be able to work you in sooner if I'm with you today."

"No favors for outsiders, huh?"

"You know small towns."

Boy, did he. That was the reason he'd stayed in Boston. "I told Granny I'd rather call someone in Athens, but she wouldn't hear of it. She'll only do business here in town. Said Arnie has done her carpet for thirty years."

"Your Granny is definitely loyal." She pointed. "There it is. Pull in the parking lot on the left."

They parked, then walked in the store. A little bell jingled to announce their presence.

"I'll be right with you," called the voice he'd heard earlier on the phone.

"Why don't you let me talk to Molly. She's in my quilting group," Lindsay said.

He didn't want her thinking he was still a helpless nerd. "I can do this on my own, Lindsay."

She shook her head.

"But thanks, anyway."

She held her hand out as if offering him the store. "Fine. Do it your way." She meandered to nearby sample books and started to flip through one.

A moment later, an attractive young woman came from the back. "Hi. Can I help you?"

"My name's Bill Wellington. I called earlier."

"The man from over in Windy Hollow?"

"No, I'm from Boston."

"Boston, Georgia? Is there such a place?"

"No, ma'am. Boston, Massachusetts."

"Ah," she said as if solving a mystery. "You didn't mention that earlier."

"I'm here to pick out some carpet for my grandmother. We scheduled an appointment for a couple of weeks out, but I was hoping we could get it installed sooner."

Her face screwed up as if she was confused. "So it's for your grandmother?"

"Yes. She lives here in Magnolia. On Main Street. Her name is Bea Wellington."

"Well, why didn't you say so sooner? Arnie can probably get out there late next week for her."

"Thank you." But it grated on him that an outsider could have such a hard time getting service.

She pointed to the showroom. "Take a look and let me know if you have any questions."

A few minutes later, as he and Lindsay searched the many books, Molly reappeared. "Oh, hi, Lindsay. When did you get here?"

"I came in with Bill. We're old friends."

"Hey, I saw you dropping off Hunter and Chase the other morning. They've grown so much and look so much like their daddy—all handsome and cute." She practically twittered.

It appeared she was very interested in Lindsay's brother.

"Yes, they're sweet boys. And they're like my own now."

Molly's smile dimmed a bit. He detected some animosity, at least from Lindsay's side.

"I think I've found some carpet that will work nicely." He pointed to a commercial grade, low-pile carpet in a neutral color. "It's inexpensive since we'll be selling Granny's house."

Molly gasped. "She's selling her house? No way."

"No way is right," Lindsay said. "She'll sell someday, of course. But I'd rather her buy something nice for now. Something she can enjoy in her old age." She glared a final warning at him as she flipped open a sample book and pointed to a plush carpet in a pale shade of green—Granny's favorite color.

"Fine. We'll compromise. Molly, we'll have the plush carpet but in a neutral beige color that will sell well." He pointed to a color in Lindsay's book called *Wheat*.

For a second, he thought he saw tears in Lindsay's eyes. But it had to have been the lighting, because the next time she glared at him, they were gone.

Molly looked from him, to Lindsay, then back to him. Apparently, she decided he was the decision maker in the situation, because she wrote up the order. He checked to make sure she'd written *Wheat* instead of *Thicket*. She had. But she didn't look comfortable doing it.

"Okay. We have you set for next Thursday for the carpet installation. Someone will be out to measure on Monday."

"Thank you," he said.

The clerk looked to Lindsay. "I'm sorry about the green, Lindsay."

"It's not your fault, Molly." She walked out the door of the store.

He found her outside in his rental car. He opened his mouth and nearly said he was sorry, but then forced it shut. He felt awful, though.

He really did need to get over the guilt of leaving Lindsay so long ago. He couldn't allow it to color his decisions.

No, he wouldn't apologize. She had no right to keep interfering. Granny was *his* family, after all.

As he turned the car toward Donna Rae's house, he remembered Granny's orders. He sighed.

"What's wrong?"

"Granny gave me strict instructions to take you out for lunch."

"No, thanks. I have leftovers at home."

"She'll fuss at me."

"She would, wouldn't she?" She laughed. "Well, why don't we stop and pick up something from Minnie's to take home for all of us to eat."

"Minnie's still in business?" Minnie's Meat and Three. It had become his favorite restaurant once he hit a growth spurt in eighth grade and couldn't ever seem to eat enough. The growth spurt continued all the way through high school.

"She's still open. I'm sure she'd love to see you."

He hadn't had Minnie's fried chicken in fifteen years. And he'd like to see her, too. "Good idea. My mouth's watering just thinking about the chicken."

As they walked in the restaurant, there was a perceptible hush, a lull in the conversation.

Lindsay realized that most people, even if they knew who he was, wouldn't recognize him. Some wouldn't even remember him.

He was so smart and good-looking. She couldn't help but wonder why he'd never married. Maybe he'd never found someone to share his passion for physics. He'd loved the subject from the time he was old enough to read—in kindergarten, according to Granny Bea. When he'd moved to town the summer after fourth grade, Lindsay often found him outside, perched in the mimosa tree, reading thick nonfiction books about atomic particles that he'd checked out from the library.

He touched her elbow and guided her to a table, acting as if they weren't the center of attention. She was afraid their appearance together might become a topic for gossip.

When they sat, he whispered, "I can't believe I decided to come here. Too many people. All staring."

"Many probably don't recognize you. They'll assume I've got a boyfriend from out of town."

"Should I stand and state my name, tell them we're not a couple? Then ask them to quit staring?" His golden-brown eyes sparked with warmth.

"Maybe once your novelty wears off, you'll have some peace."

"My novelty will never wear off. I've always been considered an oddball."

"Well, I'll be," Minnie said in her deep, husky, smoker's voice as she approached the table. "My best customer has finally come home."

"Ms. Minnie, so good to see you." He stood and hugged her, dwarfing her small frame.

"Mercy, look at you, child. You grew up into the rafters and finally put some meat on your bones."

"It was your chicken, Ms. Minnie. If it hadn't been for you, I would have been blown away by a good strong wind."

"Well, I'll make sure you get all your favorites today." She smiled at Lindsay. "Hey, Lindsay. Your regular?"

"I can't resist. And a plate for Granny Bea, as well, please. Everything to go."

Minnie hurried toward the kitchen, whistling "I'll Fly Away."

They sat in silence. She ran her finger over a split in the laminated menu. "I know you visit your granny. How come I haven't seen you in so many years?"

"I've actually flown her up to visit me more often than I've come here. And my rare trips home have been very brief." He darted a glance into her eyes, then looked away, toward the front door. "I guess we haven't run into each other."

She couldn't shake the feeling he'd avoided her.

"Well, maybe you'll see some old friends this time."

"I'm only here for Granny. But it's nice to see Minnie."

Would he have ever come to see her? "You'll have to go visit Pastor Eddie. He'd love to see you."

Minnie set two glasses of syrupy-thick sweet iced tea on the table. "On the house while you wait." She tapped Bill on the shoulder. "So, sugar, what brings you to town after all this time?"

"Granny took a fall. Broke her wrist."

"Bill Wellington, shame on you. You shouldn't wait for a crisis to make you come home," Minnie said.

"I apologize. I've been in town, but haven't made it over to the restaurant."

"I forgive you. This time." Minnie shook her finger at him. "No excuses from now on."

"He won't be able to resist your chicken now that he'll have another taste," Lindsay said.

"See," Ms. Minnie said almost like a frog croaking. "You can't resist the people who care about you."

Lindsay laughed at the sounds Minnie managed to make, as well as the look on Bill's face. Something inside fluttered. She felt...well...happy. It was almost as if she and Bill were spending time together as friends once again.

"So how long are ya staying, sugar?"

"Actually, I won't be here but a few days," he said, blowing the friendly little vision out of Lindsay's mind. "I have to get back to my classes to prepare for finals."

"Well, you be sure to stop by next time." Minnie patted him on the shoulder and walked away.

Lindsay sipped her tea. "I'm sure my family will want to see you while you're here."

"I'd like that." He stretched his arms across the back of the booth, which emphasized how large he was. "You know, I'll be glad to help you with your nephews anytime you need it, Lindsay."

"Okay." Her heart squeezed. She forced herself to look him in the eye with a smile on her face. "Thank you."

"You've been a good friend to Granny. It's the least I can do."

Yeah. A good friend to Granny. Not a word about what good friends they'd been years ago. Not a word about wanting to be her friend now. She clamped her teeth together so she could resist the urge to blurt out that he should head on back to Boston and leave them alone.

She could kick herself for letting a bit of hope creep up on her.

When they arrived back at Granny's with lunch, Lindsay, who'd been quiet the whole way home, said, "I'll help you carry this in, then I'll take mine home to eat."

He knew it was the right thing to do. The smart thing. But as she reached for her sack of food, he pulled it away from her. "Why don't you stay and eat with us?"

"I need to get home. I need to…well, I—"

As he was about to accuse her of making excuses, he noticed something out of the corner of his eye. A haze. Behind the house.

"What's wrong?" she asked.

"Is that smoke?"

She didn't answer. She took off running toward the house.

He closed the gap and beat her through the front door. He bounded to the kitchen where smoke filled the air. It rolled in plumes from a pan on the stove, the acrid smell choking him. He grabbed the handle of the pot and ran out the back door with it.

"I've got the garden hose," Lindsay said from beside the back steps as she turned the water on. She unrolled the hose and pulled it over to spray the singed food.

"I'll find Granny," he said as he rushed back in the door. He called for her over and over, but no answer. She was nowhere in the house.

He found Lindsay holding her nose as she stared into the pan. "I think it was green beans."

"The stove was set on high. She must have put them on to cook quickly, then left them. She's not in the house."

"I'm sure she walked over to Sandra's."

He wouldn't quit worrying until he actually saw her. "I'll be back. Can you see if you can figure out what I did with the food from Minnie's? I have no idea where I put it down."

She grinned. "It might be up on the roof."

He grinned in return. "Maybe we can have green beans for lunch, then."

She burst out laughing. "I'll find it. Go check on Granny Bea."

He paused for a moment. He couldn't resist smiling. She looked so young, like she had when he'd been so crazy about her. She was the first to break the connection as she turned to go back inside.

He walked next door to Sandra's back entrance. The tight clench in his jaw eased when he heard Granny's voice through the screen door. She was fine.

He knocked. "Hi, ladies."

"Oh, come in, Bill," Sandra said as she jumped out of her chair and hurried over to greet him. She gave him a fierce hug. "I'm so glad you're home to see your granny. And staying for a few days no less."

"Hi, Miss Sandra. It's good to be here."

"Come join us, son," Granny said from the far side of the kitchen table.

"I can't stay. Granny, we just got home and found your pot of beans burning."

"Oh, no." She tried to get up from the low-sitting chair.

He grasped her arm and helped pull her up. "It's okay. We took the pan outside and Lindsay sprayed water on it."

"Did it damage my kitchen?"

"Once it airs out, it'll be fine."

"Oh, dear. Let's go see."

They said goodbye to Sandra and walked back to Granny's house. Lindsay stood on the back porch with the meals from Minnie's set out on the picnic table. Hers included.

"You found it?" he asked.

"Yes, slung to the side of the front door. It sloshed around a bit, but it's still edible." She gestured to the table with a smirk on her face.

Too bad he couldn't enjoy the meal with her. Unfortunately, Granny's food fiasco only strengthened his resolve that she needed to live with him to be safe.

They ate a nice meal, but beneath the pleasant chatter lay what he knew they needed to discuss. When they had a lull in the conversation, he said, "Granny, we need to talk about the kitchen incident."

"It was a simple mistake," Lindsay said. "An accident that could happen to anyone."

He wanted to ask her if she'd ever left something cooking on high then walked next door, but it would be hurtful to Granny. "I know accidents happen, but this could have turned out tragically. What if Granny had gone to take a nap? What if we hadn't arrived when we did?"

"It's the first time it's ever happened," Granny said. "I am more forgetful these days, but I'm not usually that bad. I put the beans on and wouldn't have forgotten, but Sandra called and needed two eggs for a recipe."

"And I bet you got sidetracked talking," Lindsay said. "Could happen to anyone."

"Yes. It won't happen again. I promise I'll turn burners off before leaving the house again."

He wouldn't push, but he would go ahead and make a call

to the adult day-care center near the university. He hated to move Granny against her wishes. But maybe she'd come around soon.

"I see your brain working," Lindsay said. She speared him with an intense look. "Don't make any rash decisions. You'll see that she's fine here in Magnolia."

He wouldn't accomplish anything with Lindsay interfering. She would only keep Granny stirred up. "Lindsay, this is between Granny and me. I think maybe you need to leave."

She jerked back as if he'd slapped her. Then hurt flashed across her face. "Oh. Well." She stood and jerkily put her lunch trash in the bag. She smiled at Granny, but it didn't reach her eyes.

"Lindsay…" He didn't know what to say.

Granny patted her hand. "He didn't mean it, dear. Sit back down."

"No. I should go. I—" Her voice wobbled. "I guess I'll see you tomorrow at church, Granny Bea." She hurried into the house.

He'd hurt her. He hadn't wanted to, but it was his responsibility to protect Granny.

No matter what it took.

Lindsay made it to the front of the house, seeking refuge in her car. She was determined not to cry until she closed herself inside.

Her car wasn't there. What on earth?

It's at Donna Rae's house. Bill had picked her up.

She would have to walk to Dad's, then have him drive her to Donna Rae's.

How could Bill have asked her to leave? How dare he imply that she didn't know what was good for Granny Bea?

She stormed out of the driveway, walking toward her dad's house. She was too angry to face Bill at the moment. Maybe tomorrow.

Tomorrow. Sunday. Church. *Oh, brother.* Bill would probably show up there and she would have to face him in front of everyone in her family.

She would have to prepare so she wouldn't spout off something she'd regret. And she'd also have to come up with a new plan. Apparently, showing him Granny in action wasn't going to work.

Chapter Four

The next morning, Bill sat on the front porch swing with a cup of coffee, enjoying the cool, fresh air. His legs were so long, it was nearly impossible to actually swing, so he simply pushed back and forth with his feet flat on the ground.

He set the cup aside to send a text message to one of his graduate assistants. Granny had actually fallen at an opportune time as far as classes went. The students had a weeklong reading period before finals. His assistants could field any questions from them. But the research was another thing. They were at a pretty critical point, and he needed to be there.

The roofers would be out on Monday. The carpet installed on Thursday. Maybe that would be enough improvement to put the house on the market. They could pack the necessities for Granny to move over the weekend. Then they could get everything else once the house sold.

The screen door opened. Granny stuck her head out. "You better get moving, son."

"For what?"

"Church services."

"I'll take you whenever you're ready."

"But you're not dressed for church."

No. He hadn't attended in ages. Not since moving away. Not

since he'd had Granny around to force him to go. "I won't be going today."

"So, you still haven't let go of the past?" She came all the way outside and sat beside him on the swing.

"You know I can't really put it in words, Granny. I just don't think God cares about us like you think He does. How could He, if He let my parents die on the way back from doing His work?"

"I won't pester you. But I wish you'd go with me. I think you'd enjoy visiting with everyone."

Granny hadn't seen how the youth group kids used to tease him. How he'd never felt a part of their clique. Other than Pastor Eddie, there really wasn't anyone he'd like to see again. "I'll drive you when you're ready."

She patted his hand. "Okay. I'll be out soon."

True to her word, she came through the door about ten minutes later. He drove her to the little church he'd grown up in. He pulled up out front, helped her out, then hoping he didn't run into anyone, he walked her to the front door of the sanctuary.

Once she walked in, he hurried to the car, and he sat there a few minutes, watching couples and families walk inside together. A few elderly singles, as well. No one seemed to notice him. It was like being on the outside looking in all over again.

Moving to Boston and staying there had been a good decision. He would be glad to return home. With Granny.

As soon as possible.

As he turned to look over his shoulder to pull away, he spotted Lindsay's car turning into the parking lot.

Lindsay's car. He'd last seen it at Donna Rae's house.

Oh, no. He'd totally forgotten to take her back there after lunch yesterday. Now he felt even worse. Not only had he asked her to leave Granny's house, but he'd also left her stranded with no way to get home.

When it was time to pick up Granny, Bill pulled out front once again. He slouched in the seat as folks began to drift through the door, shaking hands with the pastor. He hated that he'd sunk so low as to skulk outside the church building. He sure hoped Granny would hurry and hop in so they could go back to the house.

As the stream of people slowed to a trickle, she finally stepped outside to greet Pastor Eddie. Bill climbed out to open her door, planning to wave to the man if he saw him. While Bill stood with the passenger door open, Granny motioned to someone to follow her. The next thing he knew, Lindsay and a crowd followed Granny down the steps.

It had to be the Jones family. He recognized Lindsay's dad, Harry, though he had aged a good deal. Gregory looked pretty much the same. Gregory waved.

Too late. Bill couldn't escape.

"Good to see you again, Bill," Harry said while shaking his hand.

Gregory, who looked a bit frazzled from trying to keep two young boys by his side, also shook his hand. Gregory introduced Chase and Hunter, then the boys ran off screeching.

"I hope you'll come have lunch with us," Harry said. "Lindsay cooks up a nice roast every Sunday. And my other boy, Richard, will be in town this afternoon."

"We'd love to," Granny said.

He couldn't believe his grandmother had agreed to go. She had to know Harry was just being polite. They might not have enough food for two more. "Oh, we don't want to barge in," he added.

"Not barging at all." Harry slapped him on the back. "We always have plenty." He looked to Lindsay for confirmation.

"Yes, plenty," she said without looking directly at him.

Great. She didn't want him there any more than he wanted to be there. "No, thanks. I think we'll—"

"Lindsay," Granny said, interrupting his refusal, "I found a bag of fabric that you left at my house. It's in Bill's backseat. Why don't you grab it now before we forget."

Sure enough, a plastic bag rested on the seat.

"Oh, thank you." She walked past him to the back passenger door and opened it.

She smelled so nice, all tropical and sweet. And her hair looked soft and touchable as it swung forward while she leaned across the seat. But she had acted so prickly since he arrived. He truly wished they could be on better terms.

His grandmother jolted him back to reality when she pinched his arm to get his attention, then opened her eyes wide, giving him a look that said *you better do what I say*. "Bill, I'd really like to go eat at the Joneses' today."

"Well, I guess if that's what you want to do…"

"Good," Harry said. "We'll see you at the house."

As Bill helped Granny into the car, Pastor Eddie walked up. "So nice to see you again, Billy boy."

Bill had forgotten about the nickname. He smiled. Pastor Eddie was one of the good memories. "Thanks. It's nice to be here with Granny."

"Well, I'll let you get to your lunch. I just wanted to say hi. I hope you'll join us for the service next week if you're still here."

"Thanks." He knew it was noncommittal, but it was the best he could do. He didn't have time to debate faith issues at the moment.

He had a family gathering to attend at the Joneses'.

When they reached Harry's house, Lindsay welcomed them in. "Richard arrived right before we did. He's looking forward to seeing you."

He and Richard met up in the dining room. It was strange to see him since Richard had been only sixteen when Bill moved away. He was definitely a grown man now. Taller than his dad and brother. And looking exactly like photos of his blond-haired, blue-eyed mother.

They all settled at the table. Harry said a blessing, and then they passed the serving dishes. Somehow, they managed to have enough food for everyone. When it was time for dessert,

Lindsay shooed the little boys outside with chocolate chip cookies in hand. Then she made coffee and served chocolate cake for the adults. She'd refused his help throughout the meal, but finally relented and let him pour the coffee.

She was extremely stubborn when it came to asking for help. It seemed she thrived on being in charge of the family, a task that had come to her at too early an age after her mother's death.

"So, Richard, I hear you're in Atlanta now," he said to her brother.

"Yes, but I'm looking to move home in the next year or so. I'm tired of the hotel business."

"What do you plan to do once you get here?"

"He's finally going to pursue his dream," Lindsay said as she smiled at her brother. She looked like a proud parent.

"I plan to open a bed-and-breakfast."

"Have you ever had experience with a bed-and-breakfast?" Granny asked.

"No, ma'am. But I've had plenty of hotel management experience. I've also corresponded with several B and B owners for advice. I've studied our town and found it's a suitable location since we're near a lake."

Hunter and Chase came flying through the dining room. Chase, several inches shorter, was running after his older brother, crying about something to do with a football, as Hunter giggled. It seemed the older one enjoyed tormenting the younger one.

"Boys, settle down," Gregory hollered.

The boys circled the table again. "But Hunter hit me with the footbaw," Chase wailed.

"Stop playing in the dining room," their dad said.

They continued running, Hunter holding out the football almost within Chase's reach, then taking off full speed again, around and around the table, despite what their dad said.

"Boys." Lindsay's shoulders heaved with a big sigh. "Your dad asked you to settle down."

The boys threw on the brakes, obeying their aunt like they would a mother.

Hunter scuffed his feet, staring at them as he walked toward his dad. "Sorry, Daddy."

"Sowwy, Daddy," Chase said, trying to mimic his brother.

"I forgive you. Now go back outside and be nice to each other." Gregory rubbed each of their heads as they passed by him.

But before they went outside, they ran over to hug Lindsay. She kissed each of them. "I love you. Now go play nicely, and we'll leave for the movie in about thirty minutes."

They squealed as they ran outside, best friends once again.

"We should be going," Granny said. "I think it's about time for my Sunday nap."

"Aren't Sunday afternoons always the best time for a little snooze?" Harry said as he rose from the table and helped Granny up. "Why don't you come visit with me for a few minutes. But I only have one recliner, so we may have to fight over it." He chuckled as he escorted Granny from the room.

Bill and the others scooted back from the table. Bill grabbed a couple of the dirty plates.

"No, leave it. I'll get the dishes." Lindsay began scraping leftover food off her plate onto another.

"You won't keep me from helping to clean up," he said.

"Uh, oh," Gregory said. "Bill is making us look bad."

"Yeah, we can't be slouches while he's here." Richard grabbed two of the serving dishes.

"Okay." Lindsay sighed. "But don't break anything."

As they cleaned the dinner dishes and then the kitchen, Bill couldn't remember a time he'd had so much fun. It was like being part of a big family. It made him miss his brother all the more.

Drake was a photographer who spent more time abroad than at home. Maybe that year, the three of them could actually spend Christmas together.

He dried his hands. "Well, Granny and I need to go. You and the boys don't want to be late to the movie."

Richard slapped Gregory with a towel. "Are you going with Lindsay to help with your wild hooligans?"

"No, she's taking them so I can stay home and have a couple hours of peace and quiet to work on billing. Why don't you go?"

"I wish I could. But I need to head back to Atlanta. Bill? You can't desert her, too," Richard said.

"I should probably use the time to trim the bushes at Granny's."

"She's on my list for this week," Gregory said.

"Pardon me?"

"It's his business," Lindsay said. "Landscaping and lawn maintenance."

Gregory leaned against the kitchen counter and nodded toward his brother. "Richard pays one of my crews to stop by whenever they have a little spare time. It may take a few days, but we'll get to it for you."

"It's something Gregory and I like to do for her," Richard said. "Mrs. Wellington was good to me when Mom died. I'm honored to help out."

"She was?" Bill realized how bad that sounded. "I mean, I had no idea."

"She's a good woman."

"Yes, she is," he said. "Thank you for helping out."

"Look," Lindsay said. "Even if you don't have to trim the bushes, you don't need to feel obligated to come along to help me. The boys will be fine."

He had wanted to do some work he'd brought along with him. And to try to find some wireless Internet in town. "If you're sure you'll be okay…"

"I'm sure."

But she looked hurt again. He couldn't seem to do anything right.

"Oh, come on. Neither of you guys should work on Sunday," Richard said. "A movie will be fun."

"I don't work, we don't eat," Gregory said.

It seemed Bill had been nothing but a curmudgeon since he arrived. Maybe a movie would be a good way to ease the tension between him and Lindsay. "Actually, I could go. It would be a nice change from the lab and classroom."

Lindsay smiled at him tentatively. Maybe a truce? "Okay. So, when was the last time you saw an animated movie, Dr. Wellington?"

He laughed. "Probably in the 1900s."

"Ooh, that long ago?" She gave a playful wink.

And his heart spun into a whole new orbit. How could her mere gestures affect him like that?

"I'll drive Mrs. Wellington home and get her settled," Richard said. "Y'all can go on to the movie."

"Great. Are you ready?" Lindsay asked.

"Let's go." He gestured to the hallway leading to the living room. They stopped to tell Harry and Granny goodbye, then went outside to load the boys into Lindsay's car. He hadn't been to see a movie in months. It might be fun.

But the whole way to the movie theater, the boys chattered. And the angelic-looking, carrot-topped Chase kicked the back of Bill's seat. Not intentionally. It seemed as if he had to swing his feet to keep his dialogue going. Each time he quit talking, the kicking ceased. But each lapse in his babble only lasted about three seconds.

When they arrived, Bill bought the tickets, then sent everyone to find seats while he went to purchase popcorn packs for the children. He was trying to balance everything when a stranger walked up and put her hand on his arm.

"Well, if it isn't Bill Wellington. I'm glad I got to see you. My, if you haven't grown up!"

His synapses fired at full speed, and yet he still couldn't place the woman. "I'm sorry…"

"It's me. Donna Rae."

Oh, no. He'd been gone from Magnolia so long he hadn't recognized her at all. "Oh, hi, Donna Rae." He smiled. "How are you?"

"I'm doing great. How 'bout you?"

"Fine. I'm fine." He nodded as he remembered Donna Rae from the youth group at church and also from his class in school. She and Lindsay had been friends forever.

"Lindsay said you're here to visit your Granny."

"Yes, I had to make sure she's okay. So what are you doing these days?"

"Well, I'm married and have four kids. Vinny and I held hands around The Forever Tree our freshman year, you know. So of course we ended up getting married after high school. You remember Vinny, don't you? He's a real estate agent here in town now."

How could he forget? Vinny had instigated a good many of Bill's most humiliating experiences. "Of course."

"Oh, there he is now. Vinny, come over here." She waved her arms wildly in the air.

Vinny sauntered over, cocky as ever. Only now instead of seeming manly and intimidating, he seemed, well, old. And he had a paunchy gut. And balding head.

"Vinny, you remember Bill Wellington, don't you?"

Vinny peered up and smiled. "I sure do. Good to see you again, buddy." He held out his hand.

Bill shook it, amazed Vinny didn't seem ashamed of himself for the way he had acted as a kid. "Good to see you, too. I hear you and Donna Rae have four children. Congratulations."

"Thank you. We're really blessed." He winked at his wife.

"We've heard about you and all those degrees," Donna Rae said. "We're real proud of you up there teaching at that big-time university. Vinny's always telling everyone that we went to school with you, and how smart you were and all."

Vinny turned red. "Yeah, we're real proud of you. I know we used to tease you some. But we always knew you'd make good when you grew up. You proved us right."

"Thank you." Bill didn't really know what to say. He had a hard time digesting all the couple had said. It made no sense in light of past experiences.

"Well, we need to let you get to your movie," Vinny said. He glanced at the kid packs in Bill's hands. "Who're you here with? You got kids?"

"Oh, I'm here with Lindsay. We brought Gregory's two boys."

Donna Rae clapped her hands and nearly jumped up and down. "Oh, whadaya know! I always knew you two would get together." She gave her husband a friendly punch in the arm. "See. I told you I got chill bumps when Lindsay mentioned his name!"

"Well, that's mighty good. I'm happy for you both," Vinny said before Bill could correct their misimpression. "We'll see you around, buddy." He slapped Bill on the back and led his wife away. They snuggled up like a couple of newlyweds.

Bill felt as if he'd been dropped into some parallel universe where nothing was as it had always seemed.

Lindsay was ready to search for Bill when he finally showed up with the popcorn. He passed the boys their food, then sat beside her.

"Where on earth were you?" she whispered.

"Talking to Donna Rae and Vinny."

She nodded. "And how did that go?"

"Weird," he said. "I'll tell you about it later."

The movie seemed to drag on forever because Lindsay was so curious about the conversation. Vinny had been one of Bill's main antagonizers at church and school, so she hoped Bill was okay. Of course, Vinny had grown up a lot and was a great guy now.

When they finally left the theater, the light nearly blinded her as they walked into the lobby. She glanced around to make sure the couple wasn't anywhere nearby. "So tell me about your conversation."

"Can we have fifty cents for a video game, Aunt Lindsay? Please?"

"Sure, honey." Before she could open her purse, Bill handed them all the change he had.

"It was so strange. First, I didn't recognize Donna Rae. Then she called Vinny over. I expected him to be sheepish about his past behavior. But he wasn't. He did mention the teasing, but made it sound minor. He was even complimentary. Said he was proud of my making something out of myself."

"They are a really nice couple. It's funny how people grow up and change."

"Yeah. Maybe the memories, the bad ones anyway, can get magnified through the years."

The boys came running back. They were so young, it hadn't taken them more than thirty seconds to lose the games that were made for older kids.

"I've gotta go potty," Chase said.

Bill looked at Lindsay with a rather frantic expression.

She laughed. "Never fear. I've still got potty duty at his age. We'll be back."

When they returned, Bill was standing behind Hunter, trying to teach him how to operate the controller on one of the games. Hunter squealed as he made more progress than before. When they finally lost, and the game ended, they all left the theater.

"That was nice of you to help Hunter."

"It was fun. I haven't played in ages."

"We should do this again. Before you leave. If you have time. If you want." She wanted to kick herself. She sounded like she couldn't form a decent sentence.

"I'd like that. If you want. But, well…"

"What is it?"

"I'm afraid Donna Rae and Vinny got the wrong idea about our outing today. They think we're dating."

She waved his concern away. "I'm sure Donna Rae, the little matchmaker, jumped right on it. Don't worry, though. They're not big gossipers."

Worn out from the movie, the boys were quieter on the way home. Bill didn't seem too worried about making conversation, either. She had a burning question, though. "How come you didn't come to church with Granny today?"

"Other than Pastor Eddie, I never had a connection with the people there."

"They're nice folks."

"I guess so. I just never fit in."

Lindsay recalled an incident involving Bill and two boys who tripped him as he walked on stage in the fifth-grade Christmas pageant.

And in high school, at youth group, he always sat off by himself, reading a book. Never playing kickball or hanging out in the parking lot afterward.

"I'm really sorry, Bill. I know you had a difficult time."

"Hey, I'm over it. But I still don't relish the thought of seeing those people again."

"I guess not." But what about her? Had he dreaded seeing her again, too?

Well, no matter. He would be going back to Boston soon anyway. The only thing she needed to worry about was making sure that Granny Bea wasn't with him.

And in the meantime, if she craved a friend, she could call Donna Rae.

It's not the same, a little voice tried to tell her. *You really enjoyed spending the afternoon with him. Like old times.*

She squashed that little voice back to the same place she'd always put it whenever she started to miss Bill. Some things were too far in the past to ever resurrect.

Chapter Five

Before leaving for work Monday morning, Lindsay dialed Granny Bea to touch base about their plan. So far, Lindsay had only alienated Bill, so she had to be careful and let Granny Bea do most of the convincing.

"Hello?" Bill said.

Did the man have to answer her phone now, too? "Hi, Bill. May I speak with your grandmother, please?"

"Sure. Here she is."

The phone rustled. "Morning, dear. I was about to leave."

"I wanted to check on you. I assumed you would have Bill drive you."

"Yes, I'm going to drag him along with me again today."

"Good. I think we need to refocus our plan on the kids. Especially Dylan."

"Good idea." She hesitated. "Just don't throw Mr. Kennedy at me again, okay?" she whispered.

"The man has been dying to ask you out for two years. I just helped him along."

"He was mortified. And so was I. Please don't do it again."

"Okay. I'll let nature take its course. But I'm sure I'll have something else up my sleeve by the time you get there."

Once they hung up, Lindsay rushed to her dad's house to

get the boys and drive them to day care. Gregory needed to check on some equipment and had called twice already begging her to get the boys early. But she couldn't make it in time. He'd had to drop them by Dad's.

Luckily, her dad had them outside waiting when she drove up. She buckled them in their booster seats and waved to her dad. He loved Hunter and Chase, but he was getting a little too old to deal with them on a daily basis. They were wearing him out. It looked like she would have to pick up some of the slack.

She didn't mind, though. Once again, she relished that wonderful mixture of smells of baby shampoo and little boy as she hugged them goodbye. And it was specific to them. She didn't have the same reaction with the children at the center. Sure, she felt affection for them. But not that soul-deep love like a mother would feel for her child.

Scary. Because if Gregory ever remarried, it would be difficult to let go. But for now, they needed her. And that's all that mattered.

"We're here," Granny called as they walked in the community center.

"I'm in the office," Lindsay said from somewhere in the rear of the building.

They found her in a tiny office with a pair of scissors slicing through packing tape.

"May we help?" Bill asked.

"So you're staying?"

"The roofers are at the house today. The hammering's driving me crazy. I don't mind hanging around if you need me."

"How about moving those large boxes to that top shelf?" She pointed to a spot well above her head. It would be an easy job for him.

While he worked, the front door alarm chirped to let them know someone had arrived, so the two women went out front to greet the children. Granny's excited voice carried back to him. She sounded so happy and laughed more than he had ever remembered her laughing.

But she would have volunteer opportunities in Boston where she could work with children.

"Mr. Wellington?"

"Yes?" He turned away from the shelves and found Granny's friend, Dylan. "Oh, hi, Dylan."

"I wanted to show you my picture I drew."

"I'd love to see it."

He timidly held it up, but Bill had to squat down to see. It was a drawing of two people. One was larger and had light blue hair. The other was smaller and had black hair. He'd drawn them as purple stick people, but Bill could tell they were holding hands.

"Very nice, Dylan. Who are the two people?"

"This is me," he said, pointing to the small one. "And this is my very bestest grown-up friend."

"Who is your grown-up friend?"

"Granny Bea, of course." He grinned from ear to ear. "She loves me. And she says I'm smart."

"You sure are smart. And you're lucky Granny Bea loves you so much."

"She loves you, too, because you're her kid."

She'd said that? He swallowed hard. "She told you I grew up with her, huh?"

"Yeah. She said you're her kid *and* her grandkid. She must love you thi-i-i-i-s much." He held his arms so wide he had to strain up on his tiptoes to hold the position. The drawing flapped from the fingers of one hand.

"I love her that much, too," he said.

"I gotta go help Miss Lindsay finish getting ready for art time."

"Okay. Thanks for showing me your picture."

"You're welcome."

He hurried away. A few seconds later, Bill heard him yell, "I showed it to him, Miss Lindsay. He liked it, just like you said he would."

Bill huffed a little laugh. So, Lindsay had put Dylan up to showing him the drawing, knowing how it would affect him. He had to give her credit. She knew how to work for her cause.

But why? Why was it so important for Granny to stay in Magnolia? Sure, she and Lindsay were close. But it didn't make sense for Lindsay to go to so much trouble.

There had to be more to it. And he intended to find out.

By the end of the morning session, Bill was worn-out. He didn't know how his granny did it. He didn't know how Lindsay did it, for that matter.

At the moment, though, they both looked worried. "What's wrong?"

"Mr. Kennedy never came in today," Lindsay said.

"And he *always* comes in. He hasn't missed a day that we've been open." Granny worried with the buttons of her blouse.

"Why don't you call him?"

"Lindsay?" Granny said. "Will you do that?"

"Better yet, why don't we all run over to his house while we have some time?"

They hopped in Lindsay's car and drove a few blocks to a small duplex. They knocked at the front door for a couple of minutes, then went to the back door, a sliding glass door. Bill peeked in as they knocked.

Mr. Kennedy sat on the couch with the television blaring. He probably couldn't hear them knocking. "He's here, but can't hear us."

"Thank You, Lord," Granny said as she steepled her hands together in prayer.

Lindsay pulled on the door, and it slid open. "Hello? Mr. Kennedy?"

"What? Oh! Hello, Lindsay."

Granny walked in behind Lindsay.

"Oh, Bea, you're here, too! Let me go get dressed." He darted down the hallway, spry and fit for a man in his seventies.

He was dressed in sweat pants and a flannel shirt. Apparently, he didn't consider that dressed.

Bill bit back a grin. "I guess we should wait."

"Now that we know he's okay, we can go," Granny said, her faced flushed. "I don't want to be an imposition."

"Granny Bea, you're anything but an imposition to him. He likes you," Lindsay whispered behind her hand.

"Hush, now. You don't know what you're talking about."

Bill almost told her to go for it, she deserved to find a man to go out and have fun with after being a widow for nearly four decades. But that wouldn't work unless Mr. Kennedy wanted to move to Boston, too.

He frowned. Why did things have to get more complicated?

Several minutes later, the man, who was obviously smitten with Granny, walked in wearing dress pants, a dress shirt and a sweater vest. "Now, I'm more presentable. How do you do, ladies? Bill?"

"We were worried about you," Lindsay said. "You never miss coming to the center."

"I was going to go, but, well, I wasn't sure Bea would want me to after Friday."

Poor guy.

"Consider it forgotten," Granny said. "I'm sorry if I made you feel badly."

"Oh, I'm fine. I just didn't want to offend."

"I'm not offended at all. In fact, I have to admit I was flattered. Surprised, yes. But ultimately flattered." She fiddled with her buttons again, staring at them as if they were extremely fascinating.

He bowed like a proper gentleman. "Well, then, young lady, perhaps you'd consider having dinner with me after all."

Granny appeared to drop years in age as he spoke. She lit up with smiles. Then she seemed to realize they had an audience and checked the grin. "I'd be delighted, once my company leaves."

Bill pointed a finger at her. "Oh, no you don't. You're not

going to miss out on plans because of me. I can fend for myself for a meal."

"I suppose Lindsay could entertain you for an evening," Granny said.

Lindsay looked as if she'd wolfed down too much food in one bite. "Oh, I don't think so," she choked out. "Bill's a big guy now. He can take care of himself."

Mr. Kennedy cleared his throat. "Actually, Bea, I'd love to take you to my favorite place in Athens, but I don't feel so sure of myself driving that far. Maybe Bill could drive us."

"Of course I'll drive you."

"All settled then," Lindsay said, a little too relieved.

He should probably be insulted.

"But remember we have the seniors' trip to the mountains this Thursday," she added.

"Well, how about tomorrow, then?" Mr. Kennedy said. "The sooner the better, I say." He gave Granny a flirtatious grin.

"Perfect," Granny said.

Bill looked at Lindsay. "I guess you'll have tomorrow evening off."

She leaned closer to him, then quietly said, "And I guess Granny Bea has one more good, solid reason to stay in Magnolia."

That evening, following the onslaught of after-school children, Bill dragged himself home with Granny in tow. She was as bright and chipper as she'd been that morning. He, on the other hand, wasn't. "I'm definitely not cut out for students under eighteen."

As they made dinner together, Granny said, "Do you love your work, son?"

"I do. Especially the research. I got a text message early this morning that we've had a major breakthrough in our research. And another university confirmed they'd gotten the same results a few hours later."

"Congratulations."

"We've been on this for two years. I couldn't be more pleased." He realized that he'd regained his energy merely from talking about the project. He looked forward to getting back to his lab.

"You've been so successful. And I couldn't be happier for you."

Though he had achieved a measure of success, he still had the position of department head in his sights. Only time would tell.

No matter what happened with the promotion, he knew he'd found his place—a place where he fit in nicely, where he had the acceptance of his peers. Once he had family nearby, all would be perfect.

"Do you think they would have similar positions around Atlanta or Athens?" Granny asked.

"I don't think so."

"Never mind a wishful, old woman. More than anything, I want you to be happy."

"Don't worry, Granny. I already am."

Tuesday morning, Lindsay got ready for a day at Granny Bea's and prepared to zip out the door. No way was she going to let Bill keep her away today. She and Granny Bea needed to tag team against him to prove they could manage in Magnolia.

As she reached for the doorknob to leave, the doorbell rang, startling her. She opened the front door, and two of Donna Rae's kids stood grinning with their mom behind them, holding a child in each arm.

"Hi, Auntie Lindsay!" the oldest said.

"Hi, gang. Come on in."

Donna Rae practically sparkled. "I called to check on Granny Bea. She said she has a date tonight and that Bill is playing chauffeur."

"Yes, she's finally giving Mr. Kennedy the time of day. He's been crazy about her forever."

"This is perfect. You need to go, too. A double date!" Donna

Rae held a baby in one arm and bounced a toddler in the other, but Lindsay suspected she would jump up and down and clap her hands if she could.

"I hate to rain on your parade, Donna Rae, but there's no way. I feel like he's the enemy right now."

"Oh, puleeze. He's your friend, and he could be more." She sat little Ruthy down, then squeezed Lindsay's hand. "This is meant to be."

The hair on Lindsay's scalp stood up as chills ran down her arms. Now Donna Rae had gone and passed her chill bumps to Lindsay. "Don't do this to me. I've missed his friendship, but I can't let myself get hopeful about rekindling it."

"I'm not talking friendship here. I'm talking hands held around The Forever Tree. About *love*."

"Whoa. Now you've gone off the deep end. I never loved him. He was a good friend. We did a science project together that required we measure that silly tree. Don't read so much into it."

Lindsay pulled away from Donna Rae and slung open her front door. "Now, I love that y'all stopped by to see me, but I need to go to work."

"Think about it, Lindsay."

"There's nothing to think about."

If not, then why wouldn't the stupid goose bumps go away?

Chapter Six

Lindsay arrived at Granny Bea's in record time, as if running from Donna Rae's hopes—and her own, as well.

When she pulled into the driveway, she was relieved to see Bill's car was gone. *Good. One less thing to deal with.*

In the kitchen, she found a note on the table, anchored under a salt shaker.

Lindsay,
We went to grocery store and to run errands. Be back later.
Bill

Anger made her face prickle with heat, and flashes of light sparked behind her eyes. *He's taking over my job. Probably trying to prove I'm not needed around here.*

Once the heat and sparks wore off, though, a sick hurt took its place.

He'd been her best friend. From the time she was ten years old, she'd always been able to count on him. She knew that no matter what, he would be there for her.

Until he'd suddenly just disappeared from her life. For no apparent reason. They'd had dinner one night, and then he was…gone. And the strangest part was that he'd told her he loved her as a good friend. Evidently, a perverted way of saying goodbye.

A total, permanent goodbye.

And he hadn't come home when she needed him most: the day Joey had left her standing at the altar.

She crunched up the note. If Granny Bea didn't need her for a grocery store trip today, then it would give Lindsay a much-needed opportunity to clean out the refrigerator.

Yet as she checked expiration dates and tossed jars of old pickle relish and salad dressing into the trash can, she couldn't help but wonder how he had ignored her phone call and letter right after he had moved.

Of course, she'd refused to call more than once. She figured if he wanted to get away that badly, then she would let him.

But when Joey didn't show for the wedding, she'd thought for sure he would hurry home to comfort her. Because she couldn't have ignored Bill in the same situation even if her life had depended on it.

"Bill, honey, I'm worn out. I think we've got all we need."

He studied the grocery cart. It was definitely full. More than they needed if he got his way and she went home with him. "Okay, Granny. Let's go check out."

He'd dragged her all over town that morning, then had taken her to lunch, trying to prove to her how much fun they could have together. How much she might enjoy living with him.

Apparently, all he'd managed to do was tire her out. By the time they arrived back at the house, she was nodding off.

"Time for a nap," he said. "I'll put the food away."

"Thank you, son. I need to rest for my date tonight."

The date that, unfortunately, might make it more difficult for her to move away. "So, do you have feelings for Mr. Kennedy?"

"Well, I don't rightly know. We'll see how tonight goes."

He helped her up the front steps. "You've been on your own for a long time."

"I've never found anyone who could possibly take your granddaddy's place. He was a special man."

He'd always wished his grandmother could find companionship. But now wasn't the time. Even if he did like Mr. Kennedy. Surely Granny could hold off to meet someone in Boston.

When they reached her chair, she handed him her purse and plopped down. "Be sure you wake me in time to get ready."

"I will. Sleep well."

Lindsay appeared, wiping her hands on a towel and using a forearm to brush hair back from her face. "You're back," she whispered. She pulled over the TV tray and set the remote control within reach. All of which seemed second nature—thoughtful little things she always did for his grandmother. Part of their routine together.

There would be many "little things" he would have to learn once Granny moved in with him.

"Can I help you bring in the groceries?" she asked.

"Yeah. Thanks."

They each made two trips, going around to the back door so they wouldn't disturb Granny. Once all the bags were inside, she said, "I can take it from here."

"I'll help put them away."

"You don't know where they go."

"I lived here once, you know."

"Things change. Your granny has changed." She busied herself putting away odds and ends—a roll of paper towels and a small can of chili powder—and wouldn't look him in the eye.

"I'm sorry if I stepped on your toes, here. I'm just trying to be a good grandson."

She sighed, then turned and looked at him. "I know you are. It just messed up our regular schedule. I'll survive." She looked at her watch. "I'll get out of your way. I can pick up the boys early and take them to the park."

"They'll enjoy that."

She stared into his eyes for maybe two seconds. But it seemed like ten, like slow motion.

And he felt the old magnetism return. With a vengeance.

He took a half step toward her without thinking. Then rationality returned, and he stepped back.

"Have a nice time tonight," she said as she retreated out the back door.

Oh, boy. A whole lot *had* changed. But it looked like some things would never change.

Lindsay picked up Hunter and Chase at three o'clock, took them to the park, and then left them with her dad to all putter about in the garage.

She decided to head on home to make a simple salad and maybe even watch a movie.

After saying goodbye, she drove to her house, then changed into shorts and a T-shirt. She threw together any veggies she could round up with the salad greens, poured on ranch dressing, then set up in front of the TV with a nice glass of sweet iced tea. She heaved in a big breath. "Ah…"

The doorbell rang.

"You've got to be kidding." She dragged herself up off the couch.

Lindsay opened the door. "Hi, Bill."

He noticed food and a glass on the coffee table. "I'm sorry to interrupt your dinner. But we're desperate."

"What's wrong?"

"I woke Granny late. Now Mr. Kennedy is supposed to arrive soon, and Granny needs help with her hair and makeup."

"Oh, no! I can't believe I forgot." She ran a hand through her hair, but it flowed right back into place. So shiny. So smooth. She smelled nice, too.

"Can you come help?"

"Hang on. I need to run upstairs and get shoes."

He smiled at her, trying to act charming and not like the thunderstruck geek he had become once again. "You're always worth waiting for."

She gave one short belly laugh. "Puleeze."

It seemed she still knew him well enough not to be fooled by his attempt at being suave.

She raced upstairs, ran back down with shoes on, grabbed her purse, then turned off the lamp.

"Are you ready?" He slung his arm out, gesturing toward the door, and banged his elbow into the floor lamp. The lamp rocked precariously as he tried to catch it.

Lindsay squealed and lunged for it, too.

He managed to grab it right before it hit the floor, but the shade had been knocked crooked. "Oops. Sorry."

"That's okay."

I am such a goofball. Without another word, he carefully gestured toward the door. They locked up and left the house.

As they drove through town, she said, "So what time is Mr. Kennedy coming?"

"He's going to *come calling* at five forty-five."

"So we have just under a half hour. I think we can manage."

"I really appreciate this. She seems nervous."

"I'm so happy for them. He's had his eye on Granny Bea for a long time, but she's always said she's too old for him. It took that scare with his absence to give her a little push into the dating scene."

"I imagine it's hard to date again after the death of a spouse. Or even after divorce."

"It's been four years for Gregory," she said.

"Has he started dating again?"

"No. Of course, Molly has been after him—and the boys— practically since the ink was dry on his divorce papers. But he's not ready."

"I remember her from Arnie's Carpets. She seemed nice enough."

"She is nice. Just a little too obvious with her affections. Do you remember whose daughter she is?"

"No. Should I?"

"You know her mom. Do you remember Ms. Polly?"

His mouth fell open. "No way. The grade school secretary? She actually named her daughter Molly?"

"Awful, isn't it?"

"She was scary mean."

"Yeah. I never wanted to call my dad when I was sick," Lindsay said. "She always slapped her hand on my forehead to see if I had a fever, and told me I was being a baby."

"The one and only reason I was glad to go to middle school was to get away from her."

Lindsay laughed. "Yeah, me, too."

As they circled the courthouse in town, Bill noticed the scene of one of his only fond memories of middle school. He pointed to the city park. "There's where we did that science project together in, what, sixth grade?"

"Yes, it was sixth. We had to measure the girth of two trees." *And had held hands in the process,* he resisted adding.

She jerked her eyes straight ahead and grew silent. Almost as if wanting to drop the subject.

"There's one of the trees right there. The one everyone calls The Forever Tree," he said.

"Sure is." She snapped her face straight ahead once again.

Yep. She was changing the subject all right.

He resisted smiling. "Donna Rae mentioned the tree that day at the movie theater when she told me she and Vinny had married."

Lindsay sighed. "She believes in the silly legend. But it's grown so big now I doubt anyone can reach around it anymore."

He gave her a smirk. "I don't know. I've got really long arms."

She laughed, but then she ran her hands up and down her arms as if she were cold. "So you believe the legend?"

Too embarrassed to admit he'd always hoped it was true, that he used to assume that he would marry her, he said, "I've never believed anything like that. The scientist in me, I guess."

"I used to think about it all the time when I was young. I would fantasize about being there with some boy begging me to hold hands with him." She said it in a dreamy voice, as if she'd never held hands around the tree.

"Obviously, our hand-holding didn't count."

She shook her head. "That was different."

Bill knew he wasn't the one she dreamed about, even though she had often been in his dreams. "So who was the boy in your dreams?"

"Different boys, probably a new one each week." She laughed. "I was so fickle."

He raised a brow at her. "And there I was, trying like mad to get your attention."

She frowned as she looked away, out the window. "We were friends. At least I thought we were."

"Of course we were. I guess you were my only friend. You and my brother."

"I depended on you a lot, you know. I appreciated your friendship." She turned toward him.

There was the hurt again. In her eyes. In the way she raised her chin just a notch.

But he hadn't been there for her. Not when she really needed him.

They were silent as they pulled into Granny's driveway. Once they were inside, she burst into action, leaving him behind as she and Granny did…well, whatever women did to get ready for a first date.

Amazingly, Granny and Lindsay reappeared about five seconds before Mr. Kennedy rang the doorbell, Granny smiling proudly.

"You look radiant," Bill told his grandmother as he opened the front door.

Mr. Kennedy entered, holding a bouquet of flowers. Once he spotted Granny, he seemed rooted to the floor. "Bea," he whispered almost reverently.

"Yes, Mr. Kennedy?"

Did Granny just bat her eyelashes? Surely not.

"You…" Mr. Kennedy took a deep breath. "You look spectacular."

"Thank you."

Yep. She batted her eyelashes.

Lindsay smiled at the two of them. "So do you have reservations?"

"Sure do. We need to be on our way." He still didn't move. Just stared at Granny. "I must be the luckiest man in town."

Once he declared that, he seemed to snap out of the stunned trance and looked at Bill. "Are you ready?"

"Yes, sir."

"Good. We need to go." He bowed toward Lindsay. "So glad to see you're joining us tonight."

"Oh, I'm just leaving."

"We can drop you back at your house," Bill said.

Mr. Kennedy shook his head. "No time. You can ride along and keep Bill company."

"Excellent idea, Jasper." Granny blushed at having used his first name.

"No, I have dinner waiting at home," Lindsay said with a panicked look on her face. "Drop me downtown, and I'll walk."

"I won't hear of it." Mr. Kennedy held out one arm for Granny, then hooked his other arm through Lindsay's. He winked at Granny, and the two of them looked so pleased that Bill had to wonder if they'd had it planned all along.

Before Lindsay could voice any further objection, Mr. Kennedy escorted both ladies out the door.

Since Lindsay didn't think she could just open the door and bail out, she whispered to Bill, "Drop me in town," as he backed out of the driveway.

"Don't be a party pooper," Granny Bea said.

"How did you hear that?" Lindsay asked.

"My ears still work fine." Granny Bea laughed.

Lindsay turned to the backseat and smiled at Granny Bea and Mr. Kennedy even though she wanted to fuss at them for holding her hostage.

But how could she fuss when they looked so cute together, side-by-side, all dressed up? Granny Bea with her fanciest black patent leather purse propped in her lap. Mr. Kennedy with his bright green bow tie slightly askew.

She faced the front once again, stealing a glimpse at Chauffeur Bill—with jaw set firm and tension lowering his brow into a near frown.

He didn't look much happier than she initially felt.

They didn't say much during the drive to the restaurant. But Granny Bea and Mr. Kennedy chatted, filling the silence. When they pulled up to the front of the restaurant, Bill helped the couple inside, then came back to the car. He sat in the driver's seat, staring out the front windshield. "Well…"

"I guess we have some time to kill."

"I guess you're hungry since I interrupted your dinner."

"A little. But I'm not dressed to go anywhere." Definitely not, since she'd changed into her lounging clothes, expecting to spend a nice quiet evening at home.

"How about a trip to the drive-in? We can eat in the car."

She couldn't resist the smile that tugged at her lips. "Like old times?"

His smile broke through the tense frown and changed his whole expression. "Yeah. I guess so."

They'd made a good many late-night trips for ice cream or a milk shake during midterms and finals over the years, quizzing each other by flashlight during the drive.

He turned the car around and headed back through downtown Athens.

"This is a great college town," she said. "Don't you think you could find a job here?"

"Hmm. Thinking of another way to keep Granny in Georgia?"

She laughed. If only it were that simple.

When they reached the drive-in, he slipped into a parking space. "We're here."

Once they'd ordered, she said, "So, Boston must be a wonderful city. I've always wanted to visit."

"You have? You've sounded so anti-anything-not-Georgia."

"No, I'm just anti-taking-Granny-Bea-away."

He laughed at her bluntness. "It is a wonderful city. So much history. You'll have to come see us." He caught himself frowning from thinking of having her so far away. "Soon."

He'd barely had time alone with her. Hadn't even become friends again. She acted as if she couldn't stand him. And here he was worrying about leaving again?

"I've always wanted to travel," she said.

He remembered. At least he remembered her talking about it before her mom died. "I'm glad I don't have to. Just the occasional conference presentation."

"Sounds exciting to me. But it would be tough with Hunter and Chase to take care of."

"I'm sure Gregory can find help for a few days."

"Yeah. Well, that, and I'd have to get the nerve to fly on a plane."

"You don't like flying?"

She clasped her hands together in her lap. "I've never flown at all. I'm scared to death of planes."

"Honestly, flying scares me, too."

She sucked in a breath. "Oh, the crash. I'm so sorry. I wasn't thinking about your parents."

"It's okay. Hey, if I can fly, anyone can. Or you could get a prescription for antianxiety medication like I take before the flight." He smiled, strained, because he'd never admitted that weakness to anyone but Granny.

She put her hand on his arm, a sweet, sympathetic touch. "They were missionaries, weren't they?"

"Yes, they did mostly short-term projects in the summers or during school breaks so they could leave us with Granny. They died on the way back from helping California earthquake victims. I remember that clearly because I had watched for them on the news every night."

"Did you ever see them?"

The pain washed over him as if it had been yesterday. Every

night he'd prayed for God to bring them back safely. He'd been old enough at that point to worry about them. "No. But I did see news about the plane going down before Granny could tell me. And I somehow knew it was their plane."

"Oh, no. You never told me that."

He wanted to ask her how her God could let that happen. Instead, he reached for his wallet, glad for the distraction of the arrival of their food.

As they ate, he said, "So, enough about my family. Tell me more about yours."

"Well, Dad never remarried. Richard has been too busy working to have a social life."

"And Gregory, you've told me about."

"I guess they've turned out well. Except for Gregory's wife. He didn't choose a mate very well."

And apparently Lindsay's first choice hadn't worked out, either. Which gave Bill an awful sense of relief. "It is one of the biggest decisions a person will ever make."

Her expression turned thoughtful, almost worried. "Yes. You have to be able to trust the person. And it's nearly impossible to ever know for sure."

Joey had been a fool to fall for someone else while away at college. Didn't know what a good thing he had.

"I guess you have to trust God to lead you to the right person," she added.

He simply nodded. Again, he was good at noncommittal when it came to faith issues.

"Do you really agree with me, or are you nodding because it's the easiest thing to do right now?" she asked.

He laughed, because she'd caught him. "Not much gets by you."

"For me, the problem is figuring out whether I'm following God's leading or following my own will. What do you think?"

"I don't think God really cares one way or the other. At least not where I'm concerned."

Pain flashed across her face. "When did you lose your faith?"

"I haven't really felt like God is all that involved in our lives ever since my parents died."

"But you always came to church with Granny Bea. I thought you believed in God."

"I always have believed. I think I'm more realistic now, though." And he'd wanted more than anything for God to prove him wrong. To just once make him feel like God was right there with him. But as the years passed, it had become harder and harder to see God's involvement in his own life.

Concern formed a little crease between her brows.

He caught himself before he smoothed it away. "It's okay, Lindsay."

"No, it's not. I'm worried about you."

"Let's talk about something else."

"Do you ever attend church?"

"That's the same subject. But no, it's been a long, long time since I went."

"That's what you need, then. It'll be a start. You can sing, hear a sermon, get back to the familiar—the last place you were when you felt close to God."

The thought terrified him. God might not appreciate him darkening the doors again. "I'll consider it."

"Good. Thank you."

He gathered their trash and stuffed it in the bag. "I imagine Granny and Mr. Kennedy will be ready soon."

"Thanks for dinner."

He stared into her beautiful violet-blue eyes and had a sudden longing so strong it nearly forced him against the back of the car seat. "My pleasure."

A hint of color lit her fair skin.

He needed to be careful. He couldn't let himself enjoy the meal together too much. It was a one-time deal, after all.

Lindsay's emotions were all over the place. At the beginning of the evening, she'd thought of Bill as the enemy. The man who was trying to take Granny Bea away from her. Then she'd begun to remember their friendship. To feel his pain over his parents. To want to risk being a friend to him again.

Then he'd made her feel more than mere friendship as he'd stared into her eyes.

My pleasure.

Goose bumps skittered along her spine.

But there had also been the big bomb. He had apparently lost his faith. Now she was worried about him as a friend once again.

What a roller coaster. She rubbed the back of her neck, trying to massage away the tension building at the base of her skull.

As they drove by the University of Georgia campus, passing coffee shops and restaurants, all obviously student hangouts, he asked, "Did you ever take any classes there?"

"No. After the big breakup with Joey, I stayed home and finished my degree at the community college."

"I heard about the wedding. I'm sorry."

But could he possibly imagine the humiliation of being left standing in the narthex in an expensively refurbished wedding gown with a church full of guests staring toward the back of the church, wondering where the groom was? "It was for the best. It took a while, but I finally realized that."

As they sat at a stoplight, a young couple came out of a bookstore. The woman's arm went around the man's waist, and his arm went around her shoulders. And Lindsay felt an ache in her chest, a yearning. She couldn't afford to ache for something that would never be, so she looked away.

Having Bill around was dredging up all kinds of junk. She needed to get a grip.

As street signs flashed by, she began to notice she had trouble focusing. She blinked, opened her eyes extra wide, but to no avail. "Oh, great. Everything's blurry."

"What?"

"I'm afraid I'm getting a migraine."

An hour later, Bill winced as they arrived at Lindsay's house and he saw the pain etched on her face. After she said good-night to everyone, he walked her to her front door. Her hair brushed his cheek as he reached around to help unlock the door.

"Thank you. I'll be fine from here."

He was such a cad. The woman was feeling awful, and all he could think about was how nice it had been to feel her hair against his cheek. "No, I'll get you some ibuprofen. And how about an ice pack?"

"I can do it. Really."

"Are you just stubborn or are you trying to get rid of me for some reason?"

Her eyes looked sunken, and her coloring was off. "Neither. Go on home."

"Why won't you let me help you?"

"It's not you." She closed her eyes and grimaced. "Too much to do. Can't afford to be sick."

"Maybe it'll be better tomorrow."

"Yeah."

He'd obviously been dismissed. Still, he couldn't help but worry.

He would definitely come back to check on her in the morning.

Back at the house, Bill made himself scarce so Granny and Mr. Kennedy could say good-night. When Bill came back to the living room, Granny was alone, watching television. She already had on her robe and slippers.

"Well, has Cinderella's gown turned back into rags?"

Granny practically giggled. "Luckily, my Prince Charming got me home before midnight. I stayed gorgeous until after he left."

"So you had a nice time?"

Her eyes sparkled. "The best. What about you?"

Up until Lindsay's migraine, he'd had a nice time, too. "It was fine. A little time to catch up with each other."

"Oh, dear. I hate it about the headache. She used to get them a lot, but it's been a few years since she had one."

"I'll go over tomorrow to check on her."

"That'll be nice. And I'll call Harry and Gregory. They need to know she won't be able to take care of the kids or cook tomorrow."

He helped her up, and she went to make the calls. He checked for cell phone messages and found he'd received one while he'd had his phone off during dinner.

It was one of the grad assistants checking in. They'd run into a research problem and needed his help. He'd have to call in the morning. He also needed to make a decision about when he would head back to Boston. He'd already stayed longer than planned. But there was still carpeting work to be done, and now Granny might need to work at the community center if Lindsay couldn't be there.

"I reached Harry," Granny said. "He's going to go over first thing in the morning to see how she's doing."

"Thanks, Granny."

"Well, I think I'll turn in. I'll need my energy for tomorrow if Lindsay can't make it in for work."

"I'll be there to help you. But Granny, we need to talk." He sat across from her. "I have finals next week, but I don't feel comfortable leaving you."

"Son, I've been trying to show you I'm okay on my own. I guess you haven't gotten the point."

"Here's what I'm thinking. We can pack your things on Thursday. Then, if you agree, I'd like to go ahead and take you back with me after your work on Friday."

"I couldn't possibly pack everything in a day."

"Just enough clothes for a short while. We can finish taking care of the house once school is out. We can come back and spend a couple of weeks if needed."

"Bill, honey, I hate to disappoint you. But I can't just up and go. I would need to put in notice at work. Plus, Lindsay and I have a trip to the mountains planned for the church seniors' group on Thursday."

"I know you can't imagine moving. But you nearly burned down the house. Can't you see why I'm worried?"

She shook her head. "I'm not going to Boston right now. And that's final."

Chapter Seven

Around six in the morning, the front door opened slowly. Lindsay hoped it was her dad. She sure couldn't get up and run if it weren't—she'd barely made it to the kitchen to refresh her ice during the night. And she'd been forced to sleep on the couch because she'd been too nauseated to maneuver the stairs. "Who is it?"

"Me." Her dad peeked his head inside. "May I come in?"

"Sure."

He looked at the Ziplocked bag full of melted ice on the coffee table. "Oh, baby. Does it still hurt?"

"Only like a pickax behind my right eye."

He grimaced. "Should I call your doctor?"

"Good idea. My prescription meds have expired, and the ibuprofen is barely taking the edge off the pain."

"You know he'll want you to come by the office."

"Beg for the prescription for today. Tell him I'll come by on Friday."

He grabbed the ice pack and headed toward the kitchen. "I'll call after I make you some breakfast."

"I'm not hungry."

"You've got to eat."

"Hello," Gregory called as his boys bounded into the house. "The cavalry is here."

More like the invading troops. "I'm fine. Y'all go ahead and go to work and day care."

Hunter and Chase hopped on the couch next to her. She nearly yelled with the jarring motion.

"Boys! Take it easy. Aunt Lindsay's sick," her dad said.

"Should I kiss it for you?" Chase asked, so serious and concerned.

She rubbed his hair—still standing on end since Gregory apparently hadn't wet it that morning. "That would really help." Very carefully, she leaned toward him and pointed to her temple.

Hunter rolled his eyes as Chase leaned over and placed a slobbery kiss on the side of her face. "There. All better," Chase said, repeating what she always said to him when she kissed his boo-boos.

"Thank you. I think it hurts less already."

"Is it a bad one?" Gregory asked.

"Yeah. Like the ones I had years ago."

"We'll get out of your way. Come on guys, time to go."

"I'm sorry, Gregory. I know you needed me to pick them up today."

"Don't worry about it. Dad, do you want me to drive through after I drop off the boys and bring breakfast?"

"No, I'll cook her something," he said.

She felt like she was the world's worst hostess. "No, you all go on and do whatever you need to do. I can fend for myself."

The doorbell rang.

"Grand Central Station," she mumbled.

"Maybe it's your boyfriend, Bill." Gregory smirked.

She glared at her brother as her dad answered the door.

"Bill's here," Dad said.

"And I come bearing biscuits." He held up one of Granny Bea's baskets as his eyes went straight to hers. "How's the patient?"

Something about the way he said it made her feel…cherished. Cared for.

She didn't need that feeling. She didn't need to care. He'd

be leaving soon, and she certainly didn't want the heartache that could follow losing her friend once again.

"What are you doing here so early?" she asked, not nicely, out of her fear.

"I wanted to check on you, plus you need to eat."

"Why is everyone trying to feed me?"

Bill raised his brows as he looked at Dad and Gregory. "Did I come at a bad time?"

"No, you have perfect timing," Gregory said. "I was about to leave. She's all yours." He winked at Lindsay, then herded the boys out the door.

Bill held out the basket. "I brought biscuits."

"Sounds good," Dad said. "Let's make Lindsay a plate."

Irritated that they were talking about her as if she weren't there, she snapped, "It's just a migraine. I'm not an invalid."

"You know, it would be nice if you'd let us do something for you for a change," her dad snapped back. "You're so organized and efficient that it makes us feel incompetent."

She frowned. "I don't do that."

"Yes, you do, baby. You're always in control, and I've given up on trying to pitch in to help." His face said he was sorry. But she knew he meant every word of it.

"Well…" Did she really make them feel that way?

Apparently, she did.

Bill looked as if he'd like to slink back out the door.

"I'm sorry. I'll…eat a biscuit." And maybe try to back off some. She'd been in charge of the family for so long that she hadn't realized she'd become such a control freak.

As the men set about getting her breakfast ready, and she continued to chomp at the bit to get up and help, she tried to calm herself. To let the frustration go. Because she knew she wasn't going to be able to work at the center or to attend the lunchtime meeting of their church quilting group, the Quilting Beas—named after Granny Bea. She also wouldn't be able to attend the church outreach committee meeting that evening.

She needed to make several phone calls. She was supposed

to take the refreshments for the Quilting Beas. And she needed to get someone to take minutes for her at the committee meeting. Then there was the trip on Thursday.

She seemed to have her finger in every pot and hadn't realized it.

Bill handed her a plate with a fluffy-looking biscuit, cooked to perfection. Jelly overflowed from the sides.

She was relieved to note the nausea had passed, and she actually had an appetite. "How did you know how I like it?"

"I saw a huge jar of jelly in your fridge."

"Well, it's huge because of peanut butter and jelly sandwiches for the boys. But I do love a good biscuit with butter and jelly."

"I buttered it, too."

"Thank you. I'm sorry about being so irritable."

"Don't worry. I'd be the same way."

She eyed him because she knew he probably wouldn't be. Then she couldn't resist any longer. She took a bite of the biscuit.

Her eyelids closed. "Mmm." Once she could speak, she said, "This is amazing."

"Granny taught me how to make them years ago."

"It's a lost art. I'm envious, because mine turn out like hockey pucks."

He pulled up a chair and sat across the coffee table from her. "Granny and I will cover for you today at the community center."

She started to refuse. To insist on going no matter how she felt. Instead, she clamped her jaw shut. Then she forced air past her vocal cords and managed to say, "Thank you."

"Ooh, progress."

But she was going to go even further. "Yes. And I need to…uh…ask you a favor."

He fell back in his chair with a huge laugh. The biggest one she'd heard out of him since he hit town. "See, that didn't kill you, did it?"

"No. But it may have maimed me for life." A smile made her lips twitch as she tried to suppress it.

"You name anything you want, and it's yours." He smiled at her, looking as if he trusted that she wouldn't ask for Granny to stay in Magnolia or for a million dollars or a marriage proposal.

A marriage proposal?

She swallowed hard. "I need help dealing with the senior citizens' trip tomorrow. If my vision doesn't clear, I may not be able to drive the church van."

"You want me to cancel the trip? I can call everyone for you. Or meet them at the church to let them know."

"Well…that's not quite what I had in mind."

"I do have plans to get Granny packed tomorrow. But I can probably help you in the morning."

She set the plate in her lap, the biscuit suddenly tasting like a mouthful of raw flour. "What do you mean?"

"I'm hoping to take her back to Boston with me Friday after work." He sat in the chair as if bracing himself.

She couldn't look at him. She focused instead on wiping a blob of jelly off her plate. "Does she know?"

"Yes, she knows the plan. Of course, she refused."

She looked him in the eye once again. "Are you going to make her go?"

"I've never in my life disobeyed her. I may have to make the tough decision to move her for her own safety, though."

She had been about to ask him to drive the van on the senior trip. Maybe she should cancel it. But so many were counting on it.

And it could end up being their last-ditch effort to make Bill see Granny belonged in Magnolia.

"Will you drive for the trip to the mountains tomorrow?"

"You want me to go on the trip? To the mountains? With a church group?"

"Yes. Even if I can't drive, I'll go with you."

"How long would we be gone?"

"Leave at 8:00 a.m., get back around five o'clock. You know

if you stay around the house, you'll be in the way of the carpet layers." She could tell he wanted to say no, and enjoyed seeing him squirm.

"Are you doing this because you're trying to get me back into church involvement?"

"No. I hadn't even thought of that." A slow smile lifted the corners of her mouth. "But I like the idea."

"Well, I guess there isn't much difference between arriving back in Boston late Friday night and arriving sometime Saturday."

She nodded, knowing she had him.

"Okay. I'll go. It's the least I can do for Granny and her friends." He dragged his gaze away and focused on reaching for her plate. "And for you."

Oh, my. "Thank you, Bill." She maintained her hold on one side of the plate as he took hold of the other. It was almost as if there were a connection through the dish, as if she could sense holding his hand. Like he'd held her hand so many years ago around that tree.

He took the plate from her and stood. "Well, I need to take Granny to work. Never thought I'd be saying those words about a woman in her eighties."

She laughed as she mashed the heel of her hand against her throbbing eyebrow. "Think how long it's extending her life to have something to get up for each day."

Being stuck on the couch all day drove Lindsay up the wall. She made the phone calls to turn her church duties over to others. And after thinking about what her dad had said, she called Pastor Eddie to ask to be taken off two committees. She'd only agreed to head them up because no one else wanted to at the time. Well, someone would fill the vacancies. Maybe she'd jumped in too many times when there was someone else ready to step forward who just needed a little encouragement.

Pastor Eddie was understanding and praised her for taking some time for herself.

As if she had a life.

She picked up the phone to bug Donna Rae for a while since it was probably afternoon nap time.

"Hello?" A baby screamed in the background.

"Not a good time?"

"It's never a good time around here." She laughed. Then louder, over the wailing, said, "What's up?"

"I'm at home with a migraine."

"Oh, no! Let me come over there and help you."

"No, you've got your hands full."

"I'll get a babysitter."

She stopped herself before the automatic *no, thank you* slipped out. If she was going to learn to chill out, she had to do it in every area of her life. "Thanks, Donna Rae. I'd like that."

Donna Rae hesitated. "You would? I mean—" She laughed. "Goodness, that came out wrong. I'll be there as soon as I find someone to watch the kids." She hung up before Lindsay could say goodbye.

Lord, help me to give up control to You. Help me to act in such a way that others feel needed. I've been so busy with chores and my schedule that I've failed to care for the people I love. I've worried more about getting things done than I've worried about their feelings.

A short while later, Donna Rae walked in the front door sans kids. "Oh, poor thing. You look awful."

"You know how to make a girl feel better."

"How about some new ice?"

Once again, she caught herself from dismissing the offer. "That would be great. Thanks."

Donna Rae grinned as she gently lifted the ice pack from the back of Lindsay's head. "I kind of like seeing you sit still for a moment. I can force you to talk to me—get your undivided attention for a change."

The comment caused a pang in her chest. "I'm sorry."

"Oh, don't look so glum. I was joking."

"No, it's true. And I'm sorry."

"Lindsay, honey, what's wrong?"

"I'm turning over a new leaf. I'm going to quit trying to run everyone's lives."

"What brought this on?"

"Dad. He said I always make him feel incompetent."

Donna Rae made a face that said she might agree.

"You should have seen him. He's been in and out all day. Brought lunch. Brought my prescription. Picked up the boys early from day care and brought them by to cheer me up. He promised to come back with dinner. I wouldn't be surprised if he comes by to tuck me in."

"That's so sweet. I wish I had a man to wait on me like that," she said as she went toward the kitchen.

When Donna Rae returned, Lindsay helped her place the ice over the most painful area. "Thank you."

"So, how's it going with Bill?"

Lindsay raised her brows. "We don't have to talk about Bill every time we get together. Why don't you tell me how all your children are doing instead?"

"How long is he staying?"

She shook her head at her friend's refusal to change the subject. "He hopes to go back home by Saturday, but Granny Bea isn't cooperating."

"So if he lived here, would you be interested in dating?"

"Come on, Donna Rae."

Her friend sat on the coffee table and placed a cool hand on Lindsay's arm. "This is your best friend sittin' here. Talk to me."

Donna Rae was right. Lindsay usually shut down, didn't do the "girlfriend" thing well.

Lindsay took a deep breath, and then let it out slowly. "I still wouldn't be able to trust him. But sometimes I do feel like there's something there. Some connection. I guess it's the shared history."

"It's God's plan, I tell ya."

"And that's another thing. He's lost his faith that God is involved in our lives."

"Well, that's not good. Maybe we can help him."

"I asked him to drive the seniors to the mountains tomorrow. If anyone can help him see the love of God, it'll be that group." She certainly hoped so. For his sake, of course.

"You're right."

"You know, Donna Rae, I'm really afraid he's going to take Granny Bea away, even against her will. And I can't be friends with someone who would do that to his own grandmother."

Donna Rae busied herself fluffing Lindsay's pillow and straightening magazines and books on the end table. "Well, if you ask me, and I know you didn't, but I'll tell you anyway, I think you don't give Bill enough credit." She froze midmove. "I just have this gut feeling." She started straightening again. "I'll be praying about it."

Donna Rae was quite a prayer warrior. Lindsay had no doubt that God would hear her pleas.

But how would He answer?

Chapter Eight

The senior citizens' group was punctual. They boarded the church van right on time, Bill assisting the five elderly women on a step stool as they climbed in. Two gentlemen made the trip, as well, one of them Mr. Kennedy.

It didn't escape Bill's notice that Mr. Kennedy finagled it so he sat next to Granny. The two of them chatted, Granny's eyes lively as she discussed Lindsay's absence the day before and then the kids at the center.

Once everyone was loaded, he helped Lindsay into the passenger seat. "All better today?"

"The medicine seems to be working. Thanks. Did you meet everyone?"

"Sure did. A nice bunch." And they'd been extremely friendly, grateful that he'd agreed to drive so they could make the trip.

"Bill, does your church have a seniors' group?" Sandra asked.

"Uh…" A little frantic, Bill looked to Lindsay for help.

She didn't react.

"Actually, I don't attend a church right now."

"Did you recently leave one?" Sandra prodded.

Lindsay looked at him and smiled. *Smiled.*

"I've been working on him," Granny said. "But he never has found a place he likes."

Well, *finding a place he likes* was actually stretching the truth a little since he hadn't actually visited any. He felt awful that he'd put her in that position.

"That's too bad. I'm sure a congregation could really use your gifts," Sandra said.

"You know, you're right," Mr. Kennedy said. "Sure enough, we sometimes forget it's not just a place for us to get fed, but also a place for us to contribute."

"It's all about worship," a woman in the back said. "It's about gratitude."

What did he have to grateful for, though? His parents had been taken away from him at a young age. His fellow youth group kids had either tormented him, or worse, left him out altogether. And Lindsay had fallen in love with someone else.

You had Granny, a roof over your head and food to eat, his conscience reminded him. *And a good education. Rewarding job. Success in your field.* He really did have a lot to be thankful for. But were they blessings from God?

"Yep," Mr. Kennedy said, almost as if he'd read Bill's mind. "It's hard for me to be thankful sometimes. When my wife of fifty years died, I wanted to be buried with her. I blamed God. But once I came out of the fog, I realized God didn't take her from me. Cancer did."

"'Rejoice always; pray without ceasing; in everything give thanks; for this is the will of God in Christ Jesus for you.' First Thessalonians 5:16-18," the same lady in the back said. "We have to learn to give praise in all circumstances."

Bill couldn't even recall her name, but her voice, her assurance, spoke to him. When she quoted that scripture, it was as if God Himself were speaking to Bill. And he wished for…for what?

"Turn right up ahead," Lindsay said. "We'll head north."

As he turned, the conversation died down, then smaller private conversations took over.

Lindsay smiled at him. He couldn't imagine what for.

You do too know. She sees how you were affected by the scripture. And she's pleased.

Well, she could be pleased all she wanted. It didn't mean he'd made some major life change. No, he liked life in the rational, scientific world just fine.

He wouldn't be going back to church any time soon.

Lindsay wanted to hug Miss Camilla for knowing her Bible so well. She thought maybe the quote had actually touched Bill. He'd kept looking in the rearview mirror as Miss Camilla spoke. His face and neck had turned red. He'd frowned.

Yep, God had reached out to Bill through Miss Camilla. *Thank you, God. Please keep speaking to him.*

When they arrived at their destination an hour or so later, Bill parked on the town square and helped unload everyone. Lindsay climbed out and said, "We'll meet back here at 11:45. Our reservations for lunch are at noon."

"Bill, honey, you want to come along with me and Camilla? We're going to visit the art booths that are set up around town."

"What about Mr. Kennedy?" he asked.

"He's going to the hardware store for a while. Not too interested in art. But we'd love for you to join us."

Lindsay almost laughed at the panic on his face.

"No, thanks. I think I'll stay here and keep Lindsay company."

Obviously, she was less of a threat than Miss Camilla and her Bible.

Miss Camilla beamed. "Well, that's the sweetest thing."

Granny Bea smiled just as big. "You two have fun."

Uh-oh. It appeared the two were imagining a match.

Once everyone left, Bill said, "Are you up to walking around, or would you rather sit on one of those benches in the shade?"

"The bench sounds good. We can people-watch."

He'd been solicitous all morning, and as they approached the bench, he held out his hand to help her sit.

Rather than refuse and come across as rude, she took it, but a little zing of alarm winged through her at the contact.

She tensed as they sat side by side on the bench under a huge oak tree.

"So…you and Granny make these group trips often?"

"We try to take a day trip quarterly. Then once or twice a year, we take a longer trip, usually three or four days."

"You know, I do remember her mentioning a trip to the Biltmore House."

"We did that last December while it was decorated for Christmas. And last spring we went to Nashville to go to the Grand Ole Opry."

"What a great idea."

"Granny Bea and I plan the trips. And we room together each time. She's so much fun."

"So you work together, travel together and spend your days at her home together while you take care of her?"

"Yes. See why neither of us wants her to move?"

They sat in silence for a while after that. She hoped he was changing his plans.

"You know, Lindsay, we can go wait somewhere air-conditioned if you'd like."

"I do hate the thought of sitting here all morning. Why don't we go check out the booths?"

"Let's do it."

Bill held out his hand to help her up.

She hesitated. Then she quickly reached for him, as if to cover up the fact she'd hesitated. "You know, I'm much better now. No special treatment needed."

But as their hands touched, he glanced into her eyes, and their gazes held.

She still had the power to launch his stomach into the stratosphere.

She looked away and broke the contact, then headed down the street at a clipped pace.

Could he possibly care for her? After so many years?

"Wait for me," he said more harshly than he'd meant. But he didn't want to have feelings for her. He didn't want to have to deal with that when he returned to Boston. It had taken him years to get over her the first time. He couldn't afford that to happen again.

Of course, she was going to be so angry with him when he left with Granny that there would be no hope of her reciprocating the feelings, anyway.

Just thinking of taking Granny away tied him in knots. It would be extremely hard to do. But he had to, for her own safety.

When he caught up to Lindsay, he said, "Do you think Granny would consider having a full-time, live-in caregiver?"

"I wish she would. But I'm afraid she wouldn't."

"I've tried hiring helpers, but she's fired every single one."

"I know. She always picked one silly fault, then let them go. I truly think she didn't like having someone else in her space."

"I suspected that."

Her shoulders sagged. "I even offered to have her move in with me. She refused."

"That's really generous. I appreciate you trying."

They meandered around town and spent the next couple hours browsing at artists' booths.

"Oh, I love this angel sculpture." Lindsay had stopped at a table with carved wooden figurines. She ran her fingers over one.

"So you still have your collection?"

"Yes, and I add to it on occasion."

"Then you have to have this, too." He took it from her and handed it to the woman working the booth. "I'll take this."

Lindsay couldn't believe he'd snatched it and was trying to buy it. "Bill, no."

"Do you want it?" he asked.

"Well…yes. But I'll buy it."

"I want to get it for you. Think of it as a birthday gift for the last fifteen birthdays I missed."

How could he say that so flippantly when it hurt her just to hear the words?

He missed my last fifteen birthdays. My good friend left me and didn't even send a card. "I'm mad about that, you know." She hadn't wanted to say anything. But, well, too late.

"Mad about me missing your birthdays?"

"Yes."

The artist handed the wrapped package to Lindsay, then gave Bill a receipt.

They walked back to the bench, and he tried to help her sit under the shade tree. "I said I don't need help."

"So, you're still mad at me about the birthdays?"

"Yes. Crazy, I know. I guess I hold grudges."

"You have every right to be angry. I can't give excuses, but I can apologize."

"It was so out of character for you. I was devastated. Especially after the breakup and I was all alone."

He stared up into the tree branches. "I'm sorry. I didn't have a choice."

Yeah. Try to push if off on someone else. "Didn't have a choice? Did someone force you to leave and stay gone?"

"No. I—" He leaned his elbows on his knees and raked his hands through his hair. "I made tough decisions. And I'm sorry I didn't handle it better."

She could only imagine how badly he'd wanted to escape Magnolia and all the cruel things the kids had done to him. But it still hurt that he'd escaped her, as well. "You can quit being so mysterious about it. I think I understand, even if I don't like it."

He jerked back as if alarmed. "You understand?"

"You always hated Magnolia." She shrugged. "I guess you couldn't get away fast enough."

He slouched against the bench. "Yeah. Can you forgive me for shutting you out?"

"Can you come home and visit your granny more often?"

He laughed. "You won't give up, will you?"

"Nope. But I can try to forgive you. I got my sculpture. We'll call it even."

They sat for a few minutes, and Lindsay saw Granny Bea, Miss Camilla and Mr. Kennedy about one block away. She had a quick opportunity to make one more plea.

"Bill, I need to ask you one more time. Then I promise I'll quit bugging you about it, because I'm trying really hard to stop controlling everything in my life."

"Okay."

"Look at Granny Bea." She pointed down the street. "She's so happy. She has her first outside-the-home job, she loves helping the children, she looks forward to these trips with her church. And speaking of church…she's been a member longer than anyone else. And she has a potential love interest for the first time since her husband died. You can't take her away from all this."

"Don't you see, I don't have any other option," he said as they neared. "She's not safe on her own anymore."

"I really don't think she'll burn something again," she said quietly, smiling at the approaching seniors as if everything were right in the world.

The gang arrived with shopping bags hanging on each arm. Mr. Kennedy carried the largest bags. Probably for the ladies.

"We had success," Granny Bea said.

"Wow. Let's get your purchases loaded." Bill took the packages from them, then leaned over to whisper in her ear. "I'm sorry, Lindsay. I can't risk it."

She wanted to growl or yell with rage against the frustration. Apparently, she hadn't changed his mind.

And she'd just promised not to talk about it again.

Chapter Nine

Bill enjoyed a nice lunch with the seniors' group. Then he drove them to a couple of antique shops outside of town before heading home.

Lindsay had been quiet. Hadn't been her usually cheerful self. She'd pulled away from him since he'd reinforced the fact that he was moving Granny.

His cell phone rang. Caller ID said it was his grad assistant.

"Do you mind answering it while I'm driving?" he asked Lindsay.

"Sure." She held out her hand for the phone. "Hello, this is Lindsay Jones taking a message for Bill."

She paused. "Oh, wow. That's great news." She listened again.

They'd probably made some breakthrough with the research. He couldn't wait to hear what it was.

"Okay. I'll tell him." She hung up and held out the phone with a big smile on her face. "Announcement, everyone," she called to the passengers in the van. "That was Bill's assistant calling to let him know they got the research grant."

The group broke out in cheers. He waited for the expected rush of excitement.

Nothing. All he could think about were practical issues, like leaving Magnolia. "Wow. I didn't think we'd find out so soon."

"Congratulations," Lindsay said.

"Well, it looks like you got your grant before I got mine," Granny said. "I'm so proud of you."

"Um. The guy said you need to be back there Monday if at all possible so they can make the announcement."

"That's no problem. I plan for us to leave Saturday."

"Us?" Mr. Kennedy said.

Oh, boy. Bill didn't know how to handle this situation.

"He's still trying to talk me into going back with him," Granny said. "But I'm not going to be able to go this time."

He looked at her in the rearview mirror. Her chin was raised high, her expression daring him to contradict her. He wouldn't do that in front of all her friends. Especially not Mr. Kennedy. She would need time to tell Mr. Kennedy herself. "I've been working on Granny, but she won't budge."

However, Granny needed to tell Mr. Kennedy and others quickly. Because they would be leaving in two days.

Lindsay woke early on Friday morning with what she hoped was the tail end of the migraine. She needed to keep the doctor appointment her dad had made, but she was determined to do something to pick up the slack for her dad and Gregory.

She grabbed the phone and dialed her brother. "Hi."

"Hey. How's the headache?"

"Hanging on. I can't pick the boys up today. I have to see the doctor. But I can cook you some dinner and leave it here for you to eat."

"No, I'm good. I've watched you make the Sunday roast so many times that I went out and bought a slow cooker like Dad's. I tossed the meat in and turned it on."

"That's good. Do you have some carrots and potatoes to add later?"

"Umm. No. I forgot those."

"Heat up some canned green beans. Hunter and Chase love them."

"Great. I can actually handle that." He laughed. "You know,

it really is time I learn to do some of this stuff. Maybe you can help me."

"I'll be glad to give you some cooking lessons. We can start with a shopping list, then go to the grocery store together and—"

"Stop. You're taking over again. How about I ask you whenever I need help?"

He was right. She was at her old tactics once again. "Sure, Gregory. Let me know when you need me."

They hung up, and for some reason, she wanted to cry.

It was no fun trying to change. Especially when she liked having Gregory and the boys around.

She dialed her dad. "Good morning."

"Good morning, sunshine. Are you up and about today?"

"I'm getting there. I'm going to try going to the center this morning."

"How about I come by with some lunch?"

"I'd love that," she said without a moment of hesitation.

"See you then."

When they hung up, she took her medication, then dialed Granny Bea's house. Bill answered. Of course.

"I just wanted to let y'all know I'll be in this morning, but have to leave at noon to see the doctor."

"Is this Lindsay?" he asked in his deep voice right before he gave one of his slow, goofy chuckles.

"Real cute." She actually laughed. She couldn't help it.

"Don't come in this morning. We've got it covered already."

"But I can manage."

"You still don't sound like yourself. And the noisy kids will make it worse."

"You have a point." She had been dreading having to smile and act cheerful. "Okay. I'll take you up on the offer."

"Good."

"Hey, how does Granny Bea's new carpet look?"

"Very plush." Another chuckle.

"You're a barrel of laughs this morning, Bill." She imagined him wedged into Granny Bea's phone nook, smiling. She couldn't resist smiling, as well. "Thank you for helping at the center today."

"Glad to help. You want us to bring you some lunch?"

"No, thanks. Dad's got it covered."

"How about I stop and pick up a pizza for dinner, then?"

I? Her heart gave a flutter. Did he mean he alone? Of course he didn't.

Then why was she feeling so fluttery?

"So you and Granny Bea will both come?" she asked, just to clarify, to calm her jumpy heart.

He didn't say a word. Was totally silent.

Great.

"Yes. Both of us. We'll bring dinner after work."

"Sounds good." A friend helping a friend in need. That's all it was. But were they even friends?

"I look forward to seeing you tonight," he said, his voice deeper, more intimate than she'd ever heard it.

She drew in a voluminous breath, then let it out slowly so he wouldn't hear. But it didn't do a thing to calm her raging nerves. What could she say? *I've missed your friendship. I'm so glad you're home. I want you to stay.*

"Thanks. Bye." She hung up as soon as the words left her mouth before she could say something stupid.

Chapter Ten

Bill had almost blown it. He'd offered to take Lindsay a pizza without thinking about the fact it was almost like asking her for a date.

Sure enough, she'd caught the mistake and had corrected it, making sure Granny would be there, too.

He was such an idiot.

"What have you been frowning about, son?" Granny asked from the passenger's seat as they drove to work.

"I'm thinking about tonight. I told Lindsay we'd bring dinner."

"How nice."

"Yes, a nice friendly gesture."

"Then why the frown?"

The corners of his mouth still tugged downward, and he couldn't seem to make them stop. "No reason."

"Could it be that you're hoping to be more than just friends?" She arched a brow at him. And had a decidedly sneaky grin on her face.

"Don't go getting any ideas. I'm just being helpful."

His eyebrows joined his mouth corners in the slant downward. If he were honest with himself, he would admit he'd like it to be more.

And that wasn't good. That meant he was starting to care about her again.

They barely arrived in time to open up the center. Dylan got there about five minutes after they did, and his face was as glum as any little face Bill had ever seen.

"What's wrong, buddy?"

"I need to talk to Granny Bea."

"Okay. She'll be out in a minute. She's getting the crayons."

He sighed from the tips of his toes and leaned against Bill's side as if he didn't even realize what he was doing. Bill hesitated, then gave his shoulder a pat.

When Granny came out of the supply room, Dylan straightened. "Granny Bea. It's so terrible."

"What, honey?" She hurried to him and took hold of his hands.

"I have to move away. To live with my nana."

"For good?"

"For the summer. Mama promised I can come back here."

"I bet you'll have fun with your nana. But I'm going to miss you this summer."

He wrapped his arms around her waist. "Will you write me letters?"

Bill knew what it felt like to be thrust into an unfamiliar setting. Even though he loved Granny, it had been hard when he'd had to move to Magnolia to live permanently.

"I certainly will," Granny said. "Can you get your grandmother's address for me?"

"Yes, I'll get Mama to write it down. But I'll be back for school."

Granny looked over Dylan's head into Bill's eyes. "Yes, I'll see you then."

Once Bill and Granny finished for the day, he rushed home to change. He placed an order for carry-out pizza, then found Granny in her chair watching television.

"Are you ready?"

"Oh, you go on without me. I'm tired."

"You never get tired."

She sighed. Rather dramatically. "But I'm not usually in charge. I guess this week, with the trip and all, got to me."

Uh-oh. The room grew hotter. And so did his face. "Oh, come on. You have to eat. We'll only be an hour."

"No, you go on. Have fun." She pushed a button on her remote control until the TV reached blast level.

What could he do, haul her out the door? He pulled at the collar of his polo shirt. "I won't be long. We'll pack when I get home."

"I hope you haven't paid for plane tickets, because I'm not leaving tomorrow."

He braced for her reaction. "Yes. I purchased them earlier in the week. Then paid the fee to change them from Friday to Saturday."

"I hope they'll give you your money back."

He almost smiled. Even through his frustration, he had to admire her spunk. "We'll talk about it when I get back, Granny. I have to run."

"Don't worry about me. I'll be fine."

"No cooking, *please?* I don't want to worry."

"Okay. I'll have a sandwich. Just so you'll relax and enjoy Lindsay."

Nope. No enjoying allowed.

He kissed Granny's cheek. "See you in a bit."

"You will enjoy your date with Lindsay. There's no disobeying me on this one."

He shook his head, but gave her a smile before he walked out the door. He would not get into a discussion about what constituted a date.

Once Bill arrived at Lindsay's house with pizza box in hand, he climbed her four front steps in two strides, then rang the doorbell. He should probably be alarmed at how much he looked forward to the evening even while dreading it. Yet the most difficult part was that he would be leaving her the next day.

No answer. He rang again.

Finally, the door opened. "Come in. Oh, yummy. Pizza." She stuck her head outside and glanced around. "Where's Granny Bea?"

"She declined at the last minute. Said she was too tired."

The look she gave him said she might not believe him. But if she suspected him of plotting the whole thing, she didn't say so.

She closed the door and then headed down the entryway. "Come on back."

He followed her toward the kitchen, taking the time to check out clusters of framed family photos lining the wall. There were early photos of her mother, of the whole family at the beach, of the whole family with Pastor Eddie at a church outing, but then it was just Harry and the kids. In many of the pictures after her mother died, her dad looked sad and withdrawn, sitting in the background, unsmiling. Most of the later photos were of Lindsay and Richard. Maybe Gregory had manned the camera while their dad grieved.

Then Bill noticed the curio cabinet full of her collection of angels, the new one on the top shelf. He scanned for the one that said *I love you.*

Bottom shelf. All the way in the back.

He wasn't surprised, but it hurt, nonetheless. He hoped she hadn't noticed him looking.

They worked side by side to set the table and get drinks, then sat down to eat. He picked up a slice of pizza and sank his teeth into the gooey cheese and—

"Let's say a blessing."

"Sure." He tried not to look at her as he set it back on his plate, teeth marks and all.

It sounded as if she laughed before she said the prayer, but he didn't dare open his eyes.

"Thanks for bringing food," she said once they resumed eating. Well, he resumed. She began.

"You're welcome. I'm sorry Granny couldn't make it."

Lindsay looked sorry, too. "It's been a stressful week for her."

"She and I had a good group of kids at the center today. But Dylan told us he's moving for the summer to live with his grandmother. Granny did some checking and found out his mom is going to rehab."

"Oh, no. Not again. Was he upset?"

"Yes, and so was Granny, I think."

"They're really close. She's one of the few stable influences in Dylan's life."

"Hint, hint?"

"Yes." She smiled at him, and treated him to the full effect of her grin.

Once Bill and Lindsay finished eating, she asked him if she could go with him to help Granny pack. And to spend some "last, precious time" with her.

He felt like pond scum. "I have to warn you, she's still refusing. I have no idea what to do."

"Well, don't look at me."

Not an ounce of sympathy. As expected.

When they arrived at the house, they found the television on, but the volume lowered to a normal level.

"Oh, I love the new carpet." She kicked off her sandals, wiggled her toes, then gave him a sassy look and said, "Feels even better than it looks."

He grinned at her. "Granny, we're home."

They went to the kitchen. No Granny. "Anybody here?" Lindsay called.

Starting to worry, he said, "Let's check her room. She might be getting ready for bed."

"Sure."

They started to climb the stairs, then they heard a clunk followed by Granny's distressed cry.

Bill raced up the steps. "I think it was in the attic." He yanked open a door at the top of the steps right outside Granny's bedroom.

She was lying on the attic steps. She gripped the handrail with one hand, her upper body hanging by that one arm. His stomach hit the floor.

"Are you okay?" Lindsay yelled as they rushed to her side.

"I'm okay. Just help me get up."

He carefully placed his arms under her arms while Lindsay helped direct her feet so she could sit on the steps. Her left arm quivered.

"What happened?" he asked as he plopped down beside her. He shook nearly as badly as she did.

"I've been thinking a lot about your granddaddy. Came up here to look through some mementos. But I was getting hot and heard you calling, and as I was coming back down, I lost my balance." She lifted her right arm. "This silly cast kept me from grabbing the railing with my right hand. Thank the good Lord my left hand caught."

He thought he might be sick. He never again wanted to see her in such an awful position. "Are you hurt?"

"Only my pride."

Bill ran a hand over his face. "Maybe we should take you to the hospital."

"No, I'm fine." She rubbed her wrist with the fingers of her casted hand. "Let's go downstairs. I'm hot and thirsty."

The attic was hotter than blue blazes. His red-cheeked, sweaty grandmother was lucky they'd come home when they had.

"Here, let's help you up." Lindsay's voice shook. Then her hands shook as she prepared to help lift Granny.

Bill took hold of Granny's other arm. "Easy does it."

They helped Granny to her bedroom, supporting a good bit of her weight.

"Don't you think we should take you to the E.R. to be checked, Granny?"

"No, son. I'm fine. Just a bit weak. And glad to be cooling off."

"I'll get you some ice water," he said. "Why don't you let Lindsay help you get ready for bed?" He hesitated, looking her over for injuries.

"Bill, go get the water. I'll take care of her," Lindsay said.

* * *

Once he was out of the room, Lindsay pushed the door shut, leaving it open a crack to listen for Bill. "Are you really okay?"

"I am. My shoulder aches, but I can tell there's no real damage."

"I bet you about wrenched it from its socket."

"Oh, Lindsay, it was so awful. All I could think about was that I'm old and helpless." Granny Bea's face crumpled. "What if he hadn't been in town? You wouldn't have come until tomorrow."

"Don't even think about it."

"But the worst of it is that I know I'm going to have to move, now. I can't change his mind after this."

Lindsay shook her head as she located Granny Bea's nightgown. She walked to the bathroom to wet a washcloth, then came to stand beside Granny Bea. "Let's wash your face and hands. We'll get you a full bath tomorrow."

"I'm an old woman trying to act younger than my eighty-three years. It's time to give up, I guess."

"Move in with me. Please?"

"I won't do that to you. You've got your whole life ahead of you."

"I'd be perfectly happy to have my life with you in my home."

"You need a husband. Kids of your own."

She got that awful pang of yearning again. "Apparently, that's not in God's plan."

"Phooey."

It jolted Lindsay back a step. "Phooey on God's plan?"

"No. Phooey on you and your reasoning. Faulty reasoning."

"I beg your pardon."

"God has more in store for you than what you're living right now. I can feel it in my bones."

"You're just feeling that break in your bone." She gave Granny Bea a crooked grin as she helped her into her gown.

Granny Bea grabbed Lindsay's arm. She squeezed tightly. "You listen to me. I've been selfish. I've been enjoying your company for so long that I've held you back. And as much as your brother's children need a mother, they're holding you back, too. Gregory needs to move on and find a good woman to help raise them."

Lindsay pulled away and walked to the closet to find a hanger. "I know I need to back away from Hunter and Chase a little. But I'm not giving up our friendship. You're…well, you're like my own grandmother…and mother." Unshed tears clogged her throat. "I won't let him take you away from me." She turned around to face Granny Bea.

She looked at Lindsay with sympathy. "If Bill won't move here, then it's time for me to go."

"She's right," Bill said through the partially open door.

Lindsay opened it fully.

His head barely cleared the door frame as he walked in carrying a glass of ice water. "I don't think there's any other option this time. We're leaving tomorrow morning."

"I won't fight you anymore," Granny Bea said. She raised her chin and tried her best to look him in the eye. "But I won't go so quickly. I need you to promise me something."

Bill looked skeptical. "What?"

"I'll go to Boston with you if you'll do two things."

He raised a brow. "I won't promise until I hear them."

"One, go to church with me Sunday. And two, give me some more time. I can't leave my home on the spur of the moment."

"How much time?"

"Get someone to take over for you next week and stay to help me get ready for the move."

"So, church on Sunday, and a week to pack?"

She nodded and held out her left hand to her grandson. "So is it a deal?"

The inevitable was like a freight train bearing down on Lindsay. "Do I have any say in this whatsoever?"

"No," Granny Bea and Bill said in unison.

He shook his granny's hand. "Deal."

Chapter Eleven

Bill tucked Granny into bed. As he kissed her cheek, he took an extra moment to cherish the feel of her.

What if he hadn't been there? What if she'd been alone like that all night? She would have eventually let go. Might have fallen the rest of the way down.

He strode to the kitchen, Lindsay following, and pulled out two half-gallons of ice cream. He had to do something to take his mind off the what-ifs. "Chocolate or vanilla?" he asked.

"You can eat?"

"I have to do something to forget the image of her sprawled there, hanging on with one hand."

Lindsay sank into a chair at the table. "I can't believe this happened. She was fine last week. Now she's had three accidents in one week."

"I'm thankful I came when I did."

Her spine snapped straight like a sail catching the wind. "What's that supposed to mean?"

"Not what you're thinking. I know you've been taking good care of her."

She deflated once again. "I hate this, you know."

He put his hand over her hand and squeezed. There was no way he could see her so dejected and not comfort her. "I know. I'm sorry."

"You really are, aren't you?"

"Yes. I see how much you two love each other. It'll be hard on both of you."

He released her hand and went about making two ice cream sundaes. She never had given her preference, but he remembered that she used to love chocolate.

Neither of them spoke. But he didn't particularly feel the need to. He enjoyed her company. Even just her presence.

When the sundaes were ready, he took them to the table and sat across from her.

After several bites, she said, "I didn't mean for you to make mine. But thanks."

"My pleasure."

"So, I guess you'll have to adjust to having Granny with you."

"Not much." Although if he were totally honest, he would admit being a bit fearful.

"What about your social life?"

"I stay pretty busy at the lab."

"So you've become a workaholic?"

He sensed a trap having to do with Granny's care. "Not really. I don't work outrageous hours. But I don't socialize much, either."

"Why?"

"I've never been very social, you know that." Not that he'd wanted to be that way. Life happened to send him down that path.

"I imagine you fit in with your colleagues."

"That's true. It's been one thing I love most about my job."

She pushed the ice cream around in the bowl. "Don't you miss having a family?"

"Don't you?" he fired back.

Her gaze darted to his. "I have one —my dad, Gregory, the boys and Richard when he's home."

"I have Granny. And I'll love having her live with me."

She didn't respond other than to take a bite of ice cream with chocolate sauce.

"I'll bring her to visit you, if you'd like," he said. "And you can come see us."

She nodded with no enthusiasm at all, then reached for a napkin. The holder was empty.

He hopped up to refill it.

"I could have done that. But thanks."

"You take care of everyone else day in, day out. You need someone to do something for you for a change."

"Well, I'll be spoiled by the time you leave."

Standing beside her, he ran a finger along her silky cheek. "Good."

As soon as he'd done it, he snatched his hand away. What was wrong with him?

He dared to look at her. She stared at her bowl. She wouldn't look up.

Then it hit him. At the moment, he didn't want to leave Lindsay behind. "I'm sorry. I—"

"For what?" She looked at him and smiled as she pushed her hair behind her ear. She laughed, although it sounded a tad strained. "No big deal."

"Yeah. No big deal."

"It's the shock of Granny Bea falling," she added. "You know, the old bonding-over-a-calamity scenario."

But it had been a big deal, even though he didn't want it to be. He massaged the back of his neck. "You're right, of course."

Had he really been about to declare he was falling for her again? That he would love it if she would come to Boston with him? She obviously had no interest in him at all. Like fifteen years ago.

She pushed back from the table, then stood. "Well, I should go."

"Okay." They definitely needed to stay away from each other. He pulled out his keys.

Before he could say anything else, she took off toward the front door, leaving him behind.

The drive to her house was quiet. He didn't know what had happened that night. But everything had changed. He needed to hurry and get Granny packed and her house ready to sell so he could head back to Boston. Back to where everything made sense. Back to where he didn't feel like his very atoms were drawn to Lindsay Jones.

I cannot let him do this to me. Lindsay stared out Bill's car window. *Lord, why did You have to go and make him grow up to be so appealing? Why can't he still bumble around all the time with his nose in a book?*

He had touched her cheek, and she could still feel it.

She put her hand against the spot he'd caressed. It was warm—from her own blush at just thinking of it.

Of course, it was at that moment she realized they were passing the park. Had he slowed a little, or was she imagining it?

The shadowed outline of The Forever Tree, standing in relief with the soft glow of the moon behind it, held her gaze.

Lord, did You bring him here for a reason other than Granny Bea?

Surely not. Because I'm not going anywhere. I can't leave Hunter and Chase.

Was than an excuse, though? Even Granny Bea had told her she couldn't spend her life mothering them.

Why not? Gregory didn't have to marry again. He might be happier if he didn't.

But she'd seen how lonely he'd been. He was a great guy and would make a great husband. He had lots of love to give.

And so do I.

But her love was reserved for family. She would be safe loving them.

Bill awoke extra early Saturday morning with the need to check on Granny. It was going to take some time before he could relax about her welfare.

Once he'd been reassured by her snores ricocheting off the walls of the hallway, he tiptoed downstairs, trying to avoid all the squeaks.

He called the lab and actually caught one of his assistants there. The grad student had gone in early to set up an all-day experiment. Bill arranged for someone to cover final exams week, then they discussed the grant. Bill assured the student that he'd be back to work a week from Monday.

With cup of coffee and local newspaper in hand, he walked to the front porch swing. He snapped open Magnolia's weekly newspaper that had never been big on news. It was mostly a bulletin board for announcements, like the upcoming fund-raising barbecue by the men at Granny's church.

The paper also announced city council meetings, listed arrests—although the police blotter section was almost always blank except for when Eunice made her monthly call to the police about a Peeping Tom who was actually a figment of her imagination. The paper told about programs at the branch library and had a whole section with recipes and entertaining ideas.

Since Bill liked to cook, he checked out the recipes. He might try his hand at more southern cooking when he got back to Boston. His coworkers would be fascinated.

After scanning the recipes, he happened on a column titled "The Four Ws." He had forgotten about the *Who, What, When, Where* column. The former contributor had died about the time Bill moved away. He looked to see who the new writer was.

Polly Patton. Mean ol' Polly Patton wrote the column now?

He hated to even waste his time reading it, but like a typical rubbernecker, he couldn't resist.

Donna Rae Durante is pregnant. Again. Number five is due in the winter. Maybe Vinny should try wearing one of those pregnancy simulation suits to see how it feels to carry a baby. We wish them well.

Bea Wellington is putting her house on the market to move up north to live with her grandson, Bill. (Bill, if you recall, took off from here like a bullet the week after graduation.) Work on her house commenced this past week, starting with some roofing. Since Bea's boys have been away so long, there's a lot to be done.

And speaking of Bill Wellington. He was seen escorting Lindsay Jones at the movie on Sunday afternoon, though they were chaperoned by Hunter and Chase Jones. No word, yet, on the relationship there.

The Ladies Auxiliary at the…

Bill stopped reading. How could the town stand for the printing of petty gossip?

He didn't care a whit what Polly said about him. But he hated for Lindsay's name to be thrown in the midst of gossip. And poor Donna Rae and Vinny had their business aired for everyone to read.

That, and the paper mentioned the house being on the market when Bill hadn't even contacted a real estate agent yet.

Something he needed to do.

Vinny. He would go see Vinny this morning.

While Bill finished his coffee, Granny's car caught his attention. She'd probably had it for twenty years. *The Boat,* they'd called it. It was a monstrous sedan.

It probably had very few miles on it. And it needed to be sold. Granny shouldn't be driving.

He abandoned his coffee cup and newspaper for some paper and permanent markers from the kitchen junk drawer. While he was making a For Sale sign, Granny walked in.

"What are you doing, son?" Granny walked over and stood beside him.

"Good morning. How are you feeling?" He set the marker aside and hoped she didn't notice what he was doing. For some reason he felt guilty.

"I'm totally recovered." She looked around him. "What's for sale?"

"I'm afraid you won't be able to take your car with you when we go. I'm making a sign to advertise."

"But I like knowing I still have it. In case I ever need it."

"I'm sorry, Granny, but you won't be familiar with Boston roads or the traffic. It would be dangerous to try to drive."

"This wasn't part of the deal."

"The deal was to get you ready to go to Boston. That's what I'm trying to do."

"I won't watch while you sell off my things." She wrapped her sweater tightly around her midsection, then walked out the back door.

Well, last night he'd upset Lindsay. Now he'd upset Granny. But he couldn't let it sway his decision. He knew he was doing what was right—providing for Granny's welfare.

Everyone would simply have to adjust.

He found Granny's keys on a hook by the back door, the place she'd always kept them. He took his signs with him and taped them on the inside of each backseat window. Then, after a couple of tries, he cranked the car.

He let it run for a few minutes, backed out of the driveway, then turned toward town. He would do a little advertising on wheels.

As he drove around the town square, a few folks waved at him.

To him, it would be somewhat unnerving to live in such a small town. Any time you passed someone on the street, you most likely knew them. And they knew you. And knew your business.

He would probably have a buyer for Granny's car by the end of the day.

As he circled the square, he remembered someone had mentioned Vinny had an office downtown. He circled twice before he found it. He parked, then walked inside.

Vinny sat at a desk, talking on the phone. He waved, then motioned to a chair across from his desk.

Bill took a seat and waited.

Vinny quickly ended the conversation. "Good mornin'. What brings you by?"

"I was out taking Granny's car for a spin and saw your office. I want to put her house on the market."

"I heard you're doing repairs already."

"Yes. Roof, flooring and eventually exterior paint."

"I've got some time now if you'd like to run by and let me look it over."

It wouldn't go over well with Granny, but it had to be done. "Sure. I just need to run by the bank and get into the lockbox for the car title first. But I've got to warn you. Granny's not too happy about the move."

"From what I hear, Lindsay isn't too happy, either."

"They're both mad at me right now."

Vinny laughed. "Not a spot I envy."

"Granny still owns the house, of course. But she'll go along with the sale. She had another accident last night and finally realized she can't live on her own anymore."

"I hope she's okay."

"She wasn't hurt. And it may have been a blessing in disguise. She's finally cooperating."

"Yes, God works in mysterious ways."

He guessed his talking about a blessing in disguise led Vinny to believe he was talking about God. Well, maybe God *was* somehow working in his life after all these years.

The thought was unsettling. But in a good way. An almost comforting way.

Lindsay's phone rang as she was about to go outside to water her flowers. "Hello?"

"Lindsay, you have to get over here."

Adrenaline surged through her body. "Granny Bea, what's wrong?"

"Bill is going wild with the move stuff."

She shoved her hair behind her ear. "What's he doing?"

"He put my car—" her voice cracked "—up for sale. And now Vinny's on his way over to tromp through the house. I'm sure he's going to list it. It's too much for me to take all at once. I never dreamed he'd sell the car, too."

"Let me see what I can do. I'll be there as soon as I can."

"Thank you, dear. I knew I could count on you."

It broke Lindsay's heart to hear the normally tranquil Granny Bea upset. Lindsay had to do something. And quickly.

Think, Lindsay. Think.

She could buy the car and give it back to Granny.

Yeah, right. Like Bill would sell it to me.

Maybe her dad would buy it.

But he wouldn't want to get involved in a family matter.

No, she had to do this on her own.

She went online and looked up the value of the car, then she raced to the bank to withdraw the amount of money she needed.

Of course, it put her over her balance into her line of credit. But Granny Bea would pay her right back. The thought of Granny Bea's voice breaking drove her forward with her plan.

Once she had the cash, she called the neighbor boy who always rode his skateboard up and down the street. He was probably thirteen or fourteen, and she often hired him for little jobs around the house. His mom said he was still sleeping and had to go wake him.

"Miss J.?" he said, his voice gravelly from sleep.

"Hi, Randy. I have a quick job for you if you'd like to earn some money today."

"Cool. How much?"

She rolled her eyes. At his age, she never would have asked how much. "Ten bucks for about thirty minutes of work."

"Cool. When do you want me to come over?"

"Can you come now?"

"Be right there."

While she waited, she wrote down a set of instructions. She hoped Randy could pull this off. If not, she'd have to go back to the drawing board.

The trick would be to have him tell the truth without giving her away.

Bill stood outside Granny's house and waved as Vinny drove away. About the time he started up the front steps, a boy rode in the driveway on a skateboard.

"Hey, dude, are you the one selling the car?"

Dude? "Yes."

"I'd like to buy it."

He arched a brow. "You driving these days?"

"No. It's for my neighbor. She heard about the car and said she knew Mrs. Wellington would have taken good care of it and didn't want anyone else to buy it before she could. She sent cash." He pulled an envelope out of his pocket.

"Why didn't she come herself?"

"I don't know. Miss J. did say she's buying it for a good friend who is almost like family. A person who has always admired Mrs. Wellington's car."

"Well, who would I make a bill of sale out to? Miss Jay?"

"She said she would fill that part in when she gave the car to her friend. She said you could keep the title for now. She'll call you about that later."

"I don't suppose you're going to drive it to her home?"

The skater *dude* snorted out a laugh and gave the car a derisive look. "No way. I'm supposed to take her the keys and she'll pick it up later."

"So how much money did she send?"

He handed over the envelope.

"She must trust you a lot to let you carry this much cash." He opened the envelope and counted the bills. "This is actually a bit more than I'm asking."

"I guess I can take some back to her."

The kid seemed to be on the up-and-up. The neighbor must be an elderly woman who had trouble getting. Or was someone younger who worked on weekends.

It would make his life simpler if he didn't have to wait around for potential buyers to test drive the car.

"Okay. You've got yourself a car. Let's go inside and do the transfer."

Lindsay's phone rang for the umpteenth time that day. "Hello?"

"Lindsay, he's selling it right now."

Her stomach tightened. "To whom?"

"A kid on a skateboard, of all things."

She smiled. "Don't worry. He's my neighbor, part of my plan."

"Oh, Lindsay, honey, you're something else." She laughed, then muffled the sound as if trying to stop herself. "What on earth have you done?"

"I bought your car. We'll figure out the details later."

"You're precious. I don't know how to thank you."

"No need. I want you to be happy. That's my reward."

Granny Bea breathed heavily on the other end of the line. "Bill and Vinny talked contracts today. It appears the house will go on the market this coming week."

"I don't think I can do anything to help you there, Granny Bea."

"I know." She sighed. "Last night's scare sealed the end of my independence. But I still need your help. He'll want me to sell everything. I need you to help me figure out what to take with me up there and what to let go."

"I'll do all I can to make the move easier for you."

"So that's Plan B, then?"

"I guess it is." As depressing as the thought was.

"Well, dear, can you come over and help me sort and pack?"

Lindsay huffed. "I will, but I still don't have to like it."

"We'll start in the garage."

The messy, cram-packed garage, huh? Lindsay had promised not to talk Bill into letting Granny stay. But she hadn't promised to make the move easy for him.

Chapter Twelve

As Lindsay hung up the phone, the doorbell rang.

Before she reached the door, it burst open and Hunter and Chase barreled in.

"Hi, guys."

"Hi, Aunt Lindsay," Hunter said as he dodged her hug to run to the kitchen.

Chase wrapped himself around her legs. "I mithed you so much."

"I missed you, too, baby. But I'm all well today. Where's your daddy?"

"Outside mowing your gwass."

"How nice. I tell you what, go to the kitchen and tell Hunter there are cookies in a Baggie on the table."

He raced off while Lindsay waved out the front door to her brother. It looked as if she'd have to take the boys with her to Granny Bea's. Either that or take them by her dad's house.

No, he probably needed a break.

She went to the kitchen to round up the guys. Once they'd finished their snack, and she'd wiped the chocolate off their faces, they went out front.

By that time, Gregory had made a couple of passes across the front yard. He waved.

"We're going to Granny Bea's," she yelled over the obnoxiously loud motor.

He braked. "I'll pick them up when I'm done."

"Let me keep them today. I'll bring them to you later."

He gave her a salute as he continued mowing. "Thank you."

When they arrived at Granny Bea's house, the boys dashed around to the back. Lindsay followed them to the sandbox Granny Bea had restored for them. It had been for Bill and Drake at one time. Although, for the life of her, she couldn't remember Bill ever playing in it. She could picture Drake digging and shoveling and driving dump trucks through the sand. But Bill?

No, he'd always had a book in his hands.

"I'm going inside. You boys play nicely."

Lindsay climbed the back steps and tapped on the door as she opened it.

Bill's deep voice carried from the direction of the dining room. "Yes, this coming Friday." He paused. "Yes, I realize that."

She stuck her head around the corner. He was on the phone. He waved.

She waited, wondering who he was talking to.

"I appreciate it. We'll see you then." He hung up. "Hi, Lindsay."

"Who were you talking to?"

"The movers. I had a hard time finding someone on such short notice."

Hint, hint, she wanted to say. She managed to refrain, though. "For next weekend?"

"Friday. That way we can fly out Saturday, then be there for them to arrive on Sunday. I'll have Sunday to get Granny moved in so I can go back to work Monday."

"You have it all nice and planned out."

He looked at her. Really looked at her, eyes a bit squinted, as if he were studying her under a microscope.

But then, he didn't do microscopes. He did telescopes.

She shook her head to get her thoughts back on track.

"That sounded like a sarcastic remark," he said as he approached.

"I guess it was. I'm on edge with talk of the move."

"It's going to happen whether any of us likes it or not."

"So you don't like the idea, either?"

"I don't relish moving Granny away from her home and friends, no. But it's the right thing to do."

"Who made you the sole judge of what's right? Have you prayed about your decision?" That was a harsh thing to say, but she wouldn't apologize for the truth.

He took a step back. "I'm not the sole judge. But Granny is Drake's and my responsibility. And with him out of the country, that leaves me to make the decisions."

She held up her hand. "I'm sorry. I'm breaking my promise to leave you alone about it."

"I would appreciate a little support."

"I'm afraid you're barking up the wrong tree, there. Now..." She looked toward the family room. "I'm here to help Granny Bea pack. Where is she?"

"In the garage."

If she hadn't been so depressed, she would have laughed as she remembered their discussions about Plan B. "Good place to start."

Bill waved to Hunter and Chase as he and Lindsay crossed the backyard to the garage. He couldn't believe how much had accumulated there, even though it had been almost fifty years since Granny had moved in. Granny and Lindsay appeared fairly chipper about the whole thing until they'd spent nearly an hour sorting. Granny was overseeing it all from a lawn chair. Bill wasn't so chipper after lifting heavy equipment, moving it to the "keep" pile, then having Granny decide to put it in the "sell" pile.

"There is a lot in here." Lindsay turned in a circle.

Ancient tools and gardening items hung on the walls and

shelves. A rusty bicycle hung from a rack. A push mower sat in a corner gathering dust and spiderwebs ever since Gregory took over the mowing years ago.

"Was this your first house?" Lindsay asked.

"It was our second house. We rented a small place and saved every penny before buying this."

"It's so homey." Lindsay tossed a broken bucket into a trash bin. "A nice place for kids to grow up."

"Yes, but then we were blessed with only one child. This house felt mighty big until Bill and Drake came along."

"I guess I do take up a lot of room." He grinned at Granny. Her home and yard had been an oasis in his chaotic life. He probably loved the place almost as much as she did.

Lindsay stood in the middle of the garage and turned in another circle. "I think we're going to need more muscle to get this place cleaned out. I can get Gregory and his crew to help sometime next week or even the following week."

"After we're gone," Granny Bea said.

Lindsay looked at Bill, which increased his guilt exponentially, then she said "You know what, Granny Bea? We shouldn't worry about anything right now but the main items you want to take with you. The rest can wait."

"I can't bear to leave the place in a mess," she said.

"We're in good shape, Granny," Bill said. "We have time to pack what's important to you. We'll be flying home a week from today."

"Flying next Saturday?"

"Yes, I changed the tickets late last night. And movers are coming on Friday to load all the furniture you want to take."

Silence filled the dusty garage, a silence so thick he could almost imagine the old building breathing, groaning with age and depression.

Kind of like he felt at the moment.

Either Hunter or Chase screeched from across the yard, then Chase began to giggle.

"Come on, Granny Bea," Lindsay said. "Let's go inside and

mark everything you want to take with you. We'll put sticky notes on all the furniture that will go on the moving van."

"I won't be able to take much."

"You can take anything you want," Bill said as he helped her out of her lawn chair. "I'll move out my furniture if you like. I'm not attached to it at all."

He was offering anything she wanted.

Anything but what she wanted most: to stay in Magnolia.

Bill felt somewhat useless as Lindsay led the march through the house to tag everything that would go to Boston. She and Granny were a whirlwind as they selected furniture, then moved on to choose which china and stemware Granny would take.

"I can go get boxes," he said as they pondered the dishes in the kitchen.

"Great idea." Lindsay stuck her head into the farthest reaches of the lower corner cabinet. "Granny Bea, you probably haven't used any of this for a decade. I'd leave it."

"Okay, dear. I'm sure you're right."

"Is that U-Haul place still north of town?" he asked the back of Lindsay's head.

"Yes. You can also grab some boxes at the grocery store."

"I'll be back."

Neither woman said a word to him as Lindsay moved to the next cabinet.

"Well, I'm gone." He jingled his keys in his pocket to make sure he had them, waved to them even though they were paying him no attention, then walked out.

The boys were playing on the front porch, pushing the swing as high as it would go. The trouble was, their legs couldn't really reach, so they'd have to give it a push, then hop up for the ride, which didn't last long that way.

"Hey, want me to give you a push?"

"Yeah!" Hunter yelled with his arm pumping in the air.

"Yes, pwease," Chase said with a sweet smile and eyes sparkling. "You wide with us."

"All right, buddy." He sat in between them, gave the swing a huge push backward, then raised his legs straight out so they wouldn't get in the way as the swing sailed forward.

The squeals of delight nearly pierced his ears, but he couldn't help the smile that tugged at his lips even as his eardrums ached.

As they began to slow, he gave another big launch, sending them into another fit of joy. Before he knew it, he was enjoying it as much as they were. "Woo hoo!"

He gave them each a tickle as they traveled back and forth, magnifying the giggles. Then he began to sing "Off We Go Into the Wild Blue Yonder."

He kept them swinging for a full five minutes until his legs started to ache from holding them straight out in front of him. As the ride wound down, they started to gripe.

"Oh, man. Do you have to stop?"

"I'm afraid you've worn me out."

"One more time. Pwease."

"Okay, guys. This is it." He pushed them backward, then held that position until they started yelling for him to go. Then he let them fly forward for a gigantic last go.

Once they slowed to a barely perceptible backward and forward motion, Chase climbed up on his knees and threw his arms around Bill's neck. "That was fun. Thank you."

"Yeah, thanks, Bill," Hunter added as he held up one hand for a high five.

"You're welcome, guys." He patted their backs. As he did so, he happened to notice Lindsay at the front door, peering through the screen.

She didn't look happy.

"Sorry if we scared you, Lindsay. I was watching them."

"I know. It's okay." Then she turned away from the door. *Strange.*

"Well, I've got to go buy some boxes."

"Can we go?" Hunter asked.

"I don't see why not. Go ask your aunt."

They raced inside. A few minutes later, they ran back out the door with Lindsay's keys in hand. "She said yes!"

"But we have to take her car," Hunter said.

"Our caw seats," Chase added.

Oh, boy. What had he gotten himself into?

"What's wrong, Lindsay?" Granny Bea asked once the boys left with Bill.

She felt as if her lungs were shrinking and she couldn't get enough air.

Maybe she'd developed asthma.

No. More like an allergy to Bill. "Oh, Granny Bea, your grandson affects me in strange ways."

She raised her brows. "Pardon me?"

"My lungs!" She glanced away, then admitted in a whisper, "My heart."

Granny Bea shooed her as if she were a gnat. "Don't fight it. I've watched the two of you together, and have kept my nose out of your business. But maybe it's time to say something."

"What are you talking about?"

"You two are battling feelings that are almost palpable to those around you. Quit fighting it, Lindsay. Explore it and see what's there."

"What feelings?"

"That's for you to discover."

"Well, lovely. Why, after all those years of being single and miserable, then finally deciding single is okay, should I give a man a second look?"

Granny Bea took hold of Lindsay's wrists, her fingers warm and smooth, the edge of her cast rough and cool. "Because this is my grandson. Someone special."

"Yeah, yeah, and you're going to also say because we held hands around The Forever Tree." She sighed, an agitated sound, not a wistful one.

"You know I don't put much stock in that old tale. I believe more in prayer. But it sure is an interesting fact to note."

"So I should pray about this, I guess."

"Of course you should. God can help reveal your feelings."

"But can God keep me from *having* feelings? I don't want to see how sweet he is to Hunter and Chase. I don't want to watch him, in all his stubbornness and aggravating ways, look at you lovingly. I don't want my lungs to close off when he gets near me or to feel my face burn when he touches my cheek."

"Aa-ah-hhh." The sound climbed in pitch, then retreated back to where it started. "So he touched your cheek?"

"Granny Bea. Stop it."

She touched Lindsay's cheek right in the spot where Bill had touched it, only it felt way different. "Sweet baby, don't think about all your responsibilities, all your obligations. You need to follow your heart for a change."

"Should I follow my heart all the way to Boston?"

No. She wasn't prepared to do that. So she might as well not follow it at all.

Bill had been a nervous wreck when they first left the house, so sure the boys would drive him half-crazy. But they hadn't. They'd been troopers as he'd searched three different stores to find enough boxes. Now Chase's head bobbed sideways as he snoozed in his car seat on the way back to Granny's. And Hunter hummed the silly-sounding tune of some children's song.

What would it be like to have kids? To have a wife, a family?

A sudden ache zinged to his gut.

Oh, boy. Can't go there. It's too late for those dreams.

What if at some time God had had that in His plan for Bill, though? What if he'd remained true to his faith? Would God have rewarded him with a wife and family?

Was there someone out there right now that God had planned for Bill? But he'd missed the boat?

Lindsay even?

He sure was thinking about God a lot lately. Being back in Magnolia was having strange effects on him.

Rejoice always; pray without ceasing; in everything give thanks; for this is the will of God in Christ Jesus for you.

Miss Camilla's scripture verse from the mountain trip kept circulating through his head. He'd never been one for memorizing Bible verses, but for some reason, this one had stuck after only hearing it that once.

Was God trying to tell him something, maybe about His will?

Lindsay said he should pray about his decision to move Granny. Should he pray about God's will for that situation, as well?

Well, he'd be attending church the next day. Maybe he could try praying while he was there. It had been a long time, but surely he would remember how.

…for this is God's will for you…

Yes, maybe God was trying to tell him something.

"You'll need to wake Chase up real slow or he'll be a bear," Hunter said. "That's what Daddy says."

Bill realized they were home. He'd been in his own world and didn't even remember driving through town.

Scary.

"Should we let him sleep a little while?"

"He does usually take a nap. He's such a baby."

"Run in and ask your aunt what she thinks."

He tore out of the car, proud to have such an important mission.

Bill went around and opened the car doors to keep Chase cool. When he looked up, Lindsay stood on the front porch.

She waved hesitantly. Just held up her hand and wiggled her fingers. Not overly excited to see him.

He waved back and tried not to look as thrilled as he felt. He went to open the trunk to retrieve the boxes, and to keep from staring at the vision she made with the breeze stirring her hair and the sun striking it, creating an auburn glow.

He braced his hands on the edge of the trunk, closed his eyes, and tried to block her image from his mind. He refused to love her again. Beautiful hair and beautiful eyes shouldn't sway him, shouldn't make him wish for his life to be different.

She's beautiful inside, too.

"Are you okay?"

Startled, he jerked upward, slamming the crown of his head into the trunk lid. Pain sent bright light streaking behind his eyes. He rubbed at a freshly forming knot. "I'm, uh, fine. Thanks."

Her hand fluttered against his sleeve. "Oh, your poor head. Are you sure you're okay?"

Angry at himself for being such a klutz around her, he grabbed a stack of boxes and yanked them out of the trunk. "I said I'm fine."

She straightened and took a step away from him. "You don't have to bite my head off. I was just trying to help."

Nothing had changed. He always seemed to revert to his old, awkward self every time she got near him.

"I'm sorry, Lindsay. It hurt. My head. My pride." He managed a smile to show her he hadn't meant to be short. "I'm okay. I'll just have a nice knot on my head."

Lindsay took the boxes from him and smiled back. It lit her whole face, and she looked so young, like she had in high school. Sparkling, bright eyes with just a few little laugh lines bracketing them. A face that smiled often.

"So what should we do about Chase?" he asked.

A wail erupted from inside the car. A furious wail.

The bear had awakened.

"If he goes back to sleep, can you carry him in?"

"Okay."

Hauling the boxes inside, she left him alone with Chase. He had no idea what to do.

The roars calmed to irritated cries as Chase's head thrashed side to side and he strained against the car seat strap.

Bill unbuckled him and picked him up. "It's okay, buddy, I've got you."

Chase's face was flushed and sweaty, and his eyes didn't want to open. His cries mellowed to whimpers.

Bill blew cool air on his forehead. "Let's go inside and let you lie down on Granny's bed."

Chase rested his head against Bill's chest and went back to sleep.

Something gut-wrenching tore at Bill's insides. A longing so deep he froze in place.

He clutched Chase to him as he rested his cheek against the boy's damp head.

Lord, help me.

He didn't know what he wanted. What he needed. He didn't know what to say. What to ask. He hadn't prayed in so long, he hardly remembered how to do it.

Help me.

He forced himself to walk inside, taking Chase to Granny's room. He gently placed him on the cool bed, then rubbed his back until he settled back to sleep. Bill pulled the blinds closed, and then walked out, quietly shutting the door.

Once in the hallway, he rested his back against the wall.

He really had to get a grip. He was wanting things he couldn't have and was even trying to pray to a God who didn't care about him.

How crazy was that?

The sound of voices carried up the stairs, reminding him he had work to do.

Packing. Moving. Leaving Lindsay behind.

No, those were negative thoughts. He needed to put a positive spin on the situation.

He would be moving his Granny to live with him. He would have family close to him once again. And a nice, fat grant to fund more research. And maybe, if he were extremely lucky, a promotion to department head soon after returning.

The grant really couldn't have come at a better time. The current department head had announced his retirement a few short weeks ago. The search committee had been meeting. The chair himself had told Bill he was at the top of their list.

The timing was perfect.

But he'd be leaving Lindsay in Magnolia.

And Hunter and Chase.

I've lost my mind. Voices carried up to him. He headed down the stairs to see what all the commotion was about.

Mr. Kennedy stood inside the front door with a bouquet of flowers in his hand. The grin on his face spoke volumes.

The man was completely besotted.

There's too much of that going around.

"Well, are you ever going to give them to me, Mr. Kennedy? Assuming they're for me," Granny said.

"Why of course they're for you." He blushed, then with a burst of awkward movement, thrust the bouquet out to her. "I was momentarily stunned by your beauty."

She waved off the compliment, but looked pleased.

"Hello, Bill," Mr. Kennedy said when he noticed him.

"Hi, Mr. Kennedy. You're just in time to help us—" Both women glared at him. He'd almost said *pack*. "—enjoy the nice weather."

"Mr. Kennedy—Jasper—why don't we go sit on the porch swing to visit?" Granny said.

"I'd love to." A perky Mr. Kennedy followed Granny outside.

Lindsay scowled. "Way to go. You were going to break the poor man's heart."

"Granny needs to hurry and tell him that she's decided to go."

"Let her handle it." She shook her head. "Come on. Let's finish packing the china."

"It's nearly dinnertime, and you two have made a lot of progress. Why don't we stop for the day?"

She rubbed the back of her neck. "Fine with me. I do need to take the boys home."

"Chase is asleep in Granny's room."

"Oh."

As if they'd summoned him from his slumber, the little boy's feet clomped down the stairs. "Bill?"

Lindsay huffed. "He wants you."

"In here, buddy," he called. Then to her, he said, "So why does that aggravate you?"

"Because the boys like you. You're so stinkin' nice."

He laughed, then stepped a little closer. "And that's a bad thing?"

She had to crane her neck back even farther to meet his eyes. "Yes. Because they'll get attached to you, and then you'll leave."

Aha. So she was only thinking of the boys.

Lindsay was so close. His fingers ached to touch her face again. But he absolutely could not.

Someone—Chase?—grabbed his legs, pulling his attention away from Lindsay's sad eyes. He squatted down to Chase's height.

"Are you gonna kiss Aunt Windsay like those people on TV kiss?" He squinched up his nose as if the thought was horribly distasteful.

"No, big guy. She doesn't like me too much." He swung Chase up into his arms, then handed him to his aunt.

"Why don't you like him, Aunt Windsay?"

"Oh, I like him okay. But sometimes I don't like the things he does."

"That's what Daddy says about Mommy."

Lindsay flinched. "How about you go outside and find your brother. I need to take you two home."

"Okay." He wiggled out of her arms and hurried away.

"Sorry about that," she said, looking embarrassed.

"Don't worry about it."

"Well, I guess I'll see you at church." She turned and followed Chase.

Several minutes later, he heard a car start, then honk. He didn't have to look out the front door to know she and the boys had driven away. But he felt the emptiness of the house nonetheless.

"Bill?" Granny called from the porch.

He pushed open the screen door. The "young" couple sat hand in hand on the swing. "Yes, Granny?"

"I've invited Jasper to stay for dinner."

"Oh, you two have a nice dinner together. I'll get out of your way."

"No, son. We can all eat together."

"I wouldn't dream of it."

"Well, the only way I'll let you off the hook is for you to invite Lindsay to eat with you."

"I'm sure she would refuse."

"Ouch," Mr. Kennedy said.

Bill laughed. "Yeah."

Granny shook her head. "That girl doesn't know what she wants any more than you do."

He checked to make sure he had his keys and wallet. "I'll be fine. I'll go to Minnie's, take my computer and do some work."

"Okay. Have a nice dinner, son."

He would have a date all right. With research data.

Chapter Thirteen

As Lindsay drove the boys home, she fretted over their attachment to Bill.

Who are you really worried is going to get attached to him?

Still, while he'd played with them and while he'd held Chase, the look he'd had on his face… So happy.

He deserves to be loved. The thought struck her like a voice in her head. As she parked and unbuckled the boys, the voice haunted her.

She had to get Bill out of her head.

Gregory met them at the door. "Hey, guys!"

His boys ran inside and hugged him. Chase climbed up into his arms. "We helped Bill get boxes today."

"Good for you. I'm glad you helped out."

Chase put his hands on both sides of Gregory's face, leaned in close, and whispered, "He almost kissed Aunt Windsay." Then he shivered as if it gave him the heebie-jeebies.

Lindsay wanted to sidle out the front door.

Gregory made an appropriately repulsed face. "Ooh. I bet you were glad he didn't."

He nodded, then hopped down and ran off.

"Interesting day?" he asked.

"No."

"So what's the deal?"

"There's no deal. We were talking. And I guess we were close enough that Chase thought we would kiss."

"So, would you be interested?"

"You're a smart guy. Figure it out."

"What's to figure out if you two like each other?"

"Boston. Magnolia. A million miles in between?"

"So? People do long-distance relationships all the time."

"I did. Once. Won't do that again."

"Lindsay, honey, you and Joey were kids then. The guy was a jerk. Now you're all grown-up, and Bill's a great guy."

"He left me, too, once upon a time. Little boys just grow up to be bigger boys."

Gregory tilted his head and gave her a pitying look.

She couldn't stand it. "Come on, let's go see if Dad wants to grill outside tonight."

Lord, help me to be content. Whatever my circumstances.

And she meant the prayer with all her heart. Bill and Granny Bea would be leaving in less than a week. She would know heartache, she would know grief. But she wouldn't let it steal her joy, her contentment.

Somehow, she'd get through it.

Bill woke before the sun came up Sunday, so the morning lasted an eternity. And now it was time to keep his promise to Granny.

He and Granny drove to the church together, and he helped her up the front steps. He hadn't set foot in a church building for years. And today, he couldn't escape it by sitting in the car feeling left out.

As they walked into the sanctuary, the organ began to play.

No, he couldn't hide. Today he had to face the music, so to speak.

He held tighter to Granny's arm as if he were a little boy once again, afraid to enter. Afraid of the people, and afraid of God, so big and far away, who might take away his Granny, too.

Well, today, he was a grown-up a head taller than the tallest man present. He had no reason to fear the people.

But he sensed a meeting with God.

And wasn't sure he was ready for it.

"The same pew, Granny?"

"You bet. And Mr. Kennedy is going to join us."

He gave her arm a squeeze. "I'm glad."

He escorted her down the center aisle, and wasn't imagining the heads turning, the faces staring.

At least everyone was smiling.

"Welcome home, Bill," someone called. An elderly man he didn't recognize.

He nodded each time someone spoke to them.

He couldn't help but look to the front of the church to where the Jones family always sat. And there they all were, lined up like in years past, with the addition of Hunter and Chase, of course.

As if she felt him looking for her, Lindsay turned and smiled. She waved.

He smiled back, strangely comforted by the fact that she was there.

A couple of minutes after they took their seats, the service started. During announcements, Pastor Eddie looked up from the pulpit and said, "Oh, look who's here. Bill Wellington is out there with Bea. I'm glad you were able to stay a little longer, son."

Bill smiled and gave a little wave, but his faced burned from his neck to the tips of his ears. All eyes were definitely on him now if they hadn't been before.

"I'm so proud of Bill," Pastor Eddie continued to Bill's dismay. "I recently saw where he had an article published in a professional journal. Of course I couldn't understand a word it said." He laughed. "But I know he's well-respected in the field."

The congregation clapped. Clapped! Bill wanted to crawl under the pew. Instead, he said, "Thanks, Pastor Eddie," hoping it would silence him. Luckily, it worked. They moved on to praying, singing a hymn, then to the sermon.

Pastor Eddie had really aged. His formerly jet-black hair was now salt-and-pepper, with the temples totally gray. The heavy black glasses he used to favor were now replaced with wire-rimmed frames. But he still had trouble keeping them up where they belonged. He was reaching the second point in his standard three-point sermon, when they started to slide down his nose.

Bill stifled a grin, remembering all the times the glasses had nearly slipped off the end of Pastor Eddie's nose. Bill used to lose concentration on the sermon because he always watched Lindsay as she watched the pastor's glasses. She would end up on the edge of her seat, hands gripping the pew in front of her. Then, when the pastor would finally push his glasses back up, she would sit back and heave a sigh of relief.

He chuckled. Granny gave him a dirty look. "Sorry," he mouthed.

Lindsay glanced back his way, biting the corner of her mouth, trying not to smile, it seemed. She remembered.

A punch to the diaphragm couldn't have left him more breathless.

She was so beautiful. So fun. And even though they'd never had the relationship he'd wanted, they shared a past.

Would he ever feel something like that with another woman?

He pushed aside those thoughts and focused once again on the sermon. A sermon about faith through the hard times.

Bill simply could not believe that had been today's sermon topic. Only God could have planned it. It had to be by divine appointment.

Lord, did You do this for me?

Then as surely as he knew a proton had a positive charge, he knew: God was with him. And had been with him the whole way. Even when he'd fallen away from his faith.

Bill had felt cold inside for a long time. It startled him when it seemed as if he was suddenly warm inside. He liked to imagine it was God Himself taking up residence once again.

God, I'm so sorry.

"And I feel led to read one final passage," Pastor Eddie said. He flipped through the pages as he cleared his throat.

"'For I know the plans I have for you, declares the LORD, plans to prosper you and not to harm you, plans to give you hope and a future.' Jeremiah 29:11." Pastor Eddie closed his Bible. Then for some odd reason, he looked straight at Bill.

It was a direct message from God. Bill knew it like he knew about gravity or the speed of light.

He closed his eyes and squeezed them tight to keep tears from leaking out.

Thank You, God. I do have hope. I do have a future. But only with You in my life.

The organ music began once again, and they stood to sing a hymn. His voice was rusty, but he sang out of love for God.

He didn't know what the future might hold. But he knew all would be okay.

As soon as the service ended, Lindsay's dad popped up out of the pew. "We have to hurry home to finish lunch."

"When you called to tell me not to come cook, I assumed you would order out."

He winked at her. "Come on."

They hustled away without greeting the pastor or talking with anyone else, then drove to his house.

As they neared the kitchen, she smelled beef cooking. A nice roast simmered in the slow cooker as if she'd been there that morning.

"Wow." She lifted the lid. He'd even added carrots and potatoes. She poked everything with a fork. All tender.

"You did this all by yourself? Without my help?" She felt rather sulky, not liking it one bit that he hadn't called to ask her how to do it. She'd been putting on the pot roast at 6:00 a.m. on Sundays for...well, forever.

"I sure did."

She located a bag of frozen broccoli and dumped it in the steamer, then added some water. She turned the oven on to preheat for the rolls.

"I even made dessert."

She turned around and discovered a freshly baked pie right in the middle of the kitchen table like a proud centerpiece. What in the world? It wasn't in a disposable pie pan, either. It was in a Pyrex pie plate.

"I'll say it again. Wow."

Knowing her dad and brothers didn't need her anymore added to the rawness of Granny and Bill leaving. She blinked her stinging eyes.

"We're here," Gregory called as the front door opened. Footsteps followed. Big footsteps, as well as quickly running child-size footsteps.

Gregory stopped in the doorway and sniffed. "I thought Lindsay didn't come today."

"The old man's pretty amazing, huh?" her dad said as the boys circled Lindsay's legs playing chase.

"You did all this?" Richard asked from behind Gregory.

"Yes, sir."

She pushed aside her self-pity and grinned back at her dad. His proud stance did a lot to ease her hurt. "You truly are amazing. It smells wonderful. And a pie! How did you manage that?"

"I admit I used one of those refrigerated, rolled-up crusts. But I stirred up all the other ingredients from one of your mom's old recipes."

She swallowed and nodded. Couldn't manage any words.

Bill and Granny Bea walked in the kitchen. "Lindsay, it smells wonderful," Granny Bea said.

She'd had no idea they were coming, but wasn't surprised Gregory and Richard had invited them. "I can't take a bit of credit. Dad did it all by himself today."

Bill caught her eye and gave her what almost looked like a sympathetic look. Did he know how she felt?

They gathered around the table as she set the food out. The more she watched Bill as they sat and began to pass the serving dishes around, the more she thought there was something going on. He seemed different. More animated. More involved with everyone.

He joked with Gregory and Richard. He ruffled Chase's hair. He smiled more than he'd smiled over the last few days.

And when her dad said, "Let's say a blessing," Bill bowed his head before anyone else.

Oh, my.

Her heart soared. *Lord, You reached him, didn't You? He's come back to You.*

Thank You, Lord. Thank You.

"Amen," her dad said to end the blessing. She'd been so involved in her own praise, she'd missed the whole thing.

She stared into Bill's eyes, wanting to communicate to him that she knew. She couldn't help the smile that grew into a huge grin.

He smiled back, his eyes lit from within. Lit in a way that only God could do.

Something inside her moved, as if finding its place. Like a puzzle piece. As if…as if…

Oh, my. It was as if something good happening in his life made all well in her world, as well.

"So what did you think of the sermon today, Bea?" her dad asked.

"Excellent. And so true."

"Bill?" her dad asked as he took a bite of roast and waited for his answer.

"Truthfully, it was life changing. Liberating."

Dad nodded. "I can see how it would be. I thought Pastor Eddie did a fine job."

Granny Bea began to watch Bill. Lindsay could tell she sensed the change, too. When Granny Bea raised her eyes heavenward and smiled, Lindsay knew she was praising God for the miracle that had happened that day.

That night in his childhood bed, Bill tried to relax to a serenade of cicadas and tree frogs through the screen in his window. Granny had always insisted on turning off the air conditioner at night. She claimed a body needed fresh air to sleep.

It reminded him of the many hot, summer hours he'd spent in his room reading and daydreaming.

Reading about the solar system. Reading about protons and neutrons and electrons. Daydreaming about moving away and becoming a famous physicist. Daydreaming about Lindsay.

No. He didn't need to go there.

Yes, going back to Boston would be a good thing.

Lord, please help me know for sure this plan to return to Boston with Granny is the best plan. I've been so used to heading off in my own direction, so sure of myself, without ever asking You. Show me the way.

He lay there for a good while, unable to sleep. The longer he flopped around, trying to get cool, the more the outside chirping magnified. Finally, the back and forth squalling drove him to close the window. As he stared out at a backyard bathed in moonlight, he was struck with the realization of how much work lay ahead in such a short period of time. Lindsay had helped Granny get started on the packing, but Granny wanted to look at everything, to reminisce.

Is this thought from You, God? Am I rushing her?

Maybe God was trying to tell him something. Maybe he should be more sensitive to Granny's grief at leaving.

Which made him think of Mr. Kennedy.

He would have to tread carefully there. Granny might be falling in love. He needed to watch for the signs.

Signs? As if he would know.

Wanting to caress her cheek...wanting to spend more time with her...admiring the kind things she does for others...thinking what a good mother she would be...wanting to make biscuits for her.

Wanting to make biscuits for her?

He climbed back in bed and punched his pillow into a thick, lumpy mass. Then he slammed his head into it.

The insects' wailing somehow managed to pierce through his window.

He wouldn't be getting much sleep this night.

* * *

Early Monday morning, Lindsay showered and slipped into work clothes. She also tossed some jeans and a T-shirt into a bag since they planned to spend the evening packing.

Apparently, the stress of the upcoming move was taking its toll on her. She'd overslept.

No time for breakfast. Or coffee.

She snatched up her purse and keys, then rushed out the door.

When she arrived at Granny Bea's and walked in the front door, mouthwatering smells assaulted her. "Hello, where is everyone?"

"We're back here in the kitchen, dear," Granny Bea called. She and Bill sat across from each other at the table eating breakfast.

"Have a seat and join us," Granny Bea said.

She glanced at Bill. He seemed to be focused on his food and various legal pads spread around him.

"Uh, no thanks. I need to get to the center early since I missed the last couple of days. Do you want to ride with me, or would you rather have Bill bring you?"

"You go on if you have work to catch up on. You can give me a ride, can't you, Bill?"

"Sure." He dragged his attention away from the papers. "Would you like to wrap up something to take with you, Lindsay?"

It sure smelled good. And she hadn't had breakfast. She lifted the edge of a cloth napkin covering something in a basket. "Biscuits? You got up to make biscuits this morning?"

He shrugged. "I didn't sleep well and woke early. Figured I'd do something constructive with the time. So, how about some breakfast?" He finally smiled at her, acting halfway happy to see her.

"I guess I can wrap one up to take with me."

He jumped up.

"No, don't. I'll get it."

"I don't mind." He made her a to-go breakfast bag with two buttered biscuits, and a cup of coffee in an insulated mug with lid. "Cream or sugar?"

"What would you guess?"

"Well, honestly, I thought you hated coffee. But I've noticed you drink it now."

"You're right. I did hate it until recently when I tried it with lots of cream and flavored syrup."

"We don't have any syrup."

"Actually, Granny Bea keeps flavored creamer in her refrigerator for me. I'll get it if you'll throw a couple of packets of sweetener in the bag."

"Sure thing."

She should probably stay and eat a quick breakfast instead of causing such a ruckus. But she didn't relish the idea of a cozy breakfast with Bill. It felt threatening.

I'm acting so weird.

Weird. But threatening nonetheless. Because it seemed like something she could get used to. Something she would come to need.

"Here you go. All ready." He held out her bag.

"Thank you, Bill." She took it without touching him.

"We'll see you shortly," Granny Bea said. "Oh, guess what? I had a date last night." She blushed, and tried to busy herself pressing wrinkles out of the front of her blouse.

"I suppose it went well?" Lindsay asked with a glance at Bill.

"Sure did."

"Sounds like you're not telling the juicy details."

"Sure not." She grinned at Lindsay. "Go on. We'll see you at the center."

She left the two of them cleaning up the breakfast dishes. Poor Granny Bea. She was obviously getting attached to Mr. Kennedy.

Bill pulled his car out front of the community center so he could drop Granny off. He needed to find Internet access to do some work. His assistant had called that morning telling him they needed him to review some research results before the group could move on.

"Aren't you coming in?" Granny asked.

"I thought I would find a coffee shop or bookstore with wireless Internet service. I need to check in at work."

"Oh. Okay. I don't want to keep you from your work." She looked disappointed.

"Were you needing me to help today?"

"Well, nothing urgent. You have important things to do."

"Nothing's as important as you are, Granny. What did you need?"

"I'd hoped you would spend some time with Dylan. Remember the little party we're throwing for him today?"

He sighed. He'd totally forgotten. "Okay. I'll stay this morning and get my work done at lunchtime."

She patted his arm. "You're such a dear. Thank you."

When he walked in, he caught Lindsay at one of the kids' tables, folded into a small chair, eating a biscuit. She held up her finger to stop him from passing by as she finished chewing and swallowed. "Oh, Bill. This breakfast was wonderful. Thank you."

"Anytime." Except that wasn't true. What if she wanted him to make breakfast for her next week? Next month?

Agitated at the train of his thoughts, he walked away. What was he going to do? He had a career he loved. More success than he'd ever imagined. His grandmother would be living with him soon, so he had the family he'd missed. He had a nice home in a city he loved.

But Lindsay lived hours away. And she had family tying her to Magnolia—especially her nephews.

She loved Granny. If she could ever love him, would she consider moving?

Love? How could he even consider Lindsay loving him? She'd never shown any interest beyond friendship. Any time he touched her, she withdrew.

She'd been hurt by her ex-fiancé. Then apparently she'd

busied herself taking care of her family and everyone else in town. Had she ever cared about any other man?

It seemed as if she'd gone into protect mode and was still in it.

Sounded familiar.

He started to walk back to the table. Then stopped, turned and walked away again.

"Bill? Did you want something? I'm finished eating now."

He would never know if he didn't ask. He approached once again, determined to spit it out. "Have you been in love again since high school?"

She looked shocked, then started to laugh. "I thought maybe you needed to know where a computer was."

"I'm sorry."

"No, it's okay to ask. Strange at the moment, but okay."

Her smile and gorgeous, sparkling eyes made him want to kiss her. What was wrong with him today?

"I've dated a couple of men here and there, but not for long. So to answer your question, no."

"Protecting yourself?"

She shrugged. "Not intentionally. It just sort of happened."

"Lindsay, honey," Granny called from near the entrance. "Some kids are arriving."

Lindsay tried to stand, but her knees bumped the table's edge.

"Here. Let me help." He scooted her chair back, then took her arm to help her up.

"Thanks. I guess I'm too old for this."

Once she'd reached her full height, she looked up at him, then brushed her hair behind her ear. She stood close. Too close.

He backed away. "Well, I hear we're having a party today."

"Yes, a goodbye party." She frowned. "I guess we should have had one for Granny Bea, as well. I can't believe she'll be gone. It's like losing my grandmother all over again."

Or her mother? He imagined Granny had been almost like a mother to her, as well.

"Hi, Miss Lindsay! You're back." Dylan rushed to her side and hugged her around the waist.

"Hey, there, Dylan."

"Does your head hurt?"

"Nope. I'm all better. How about helping me set up the art center?"

"My favorite!"

Lindsay smiled before she took Dylan's hand and walked away.

As the kids moved through what Lindsay called centers— little areas set up for things like art, math, writing, playing house and other various things, she nabbed Bill to help with the reading center. He read a story with any child who wanted to visit his center.

While he read to a little girl named Mary, Mr. Kennedy walked in. He zoned in on Granny in about one nanosecond. A smile lit his face, and he adjusted his bow tie. Had to look his best for Granny.

Bill pulled his attention back to Mary and the story. He didn't want to think about ending the budding relationship between his grandmother and her suitor.

He also didn't want to think about ending another budding relationship—budding from his end, anyway—before it could even get started.

Chapter Fourteen

A couple of hours later, Lindsay sat in the middle of a circle of children with Dylan practically glued to her side. "Here you go. A present from all of us." She handed him a small package.

As the children's attention remained fixed on Dylan, Lindsay glanced up at Bill.

He was watching her, not the gift opening.

Her stomach did a nosedive before returning to where it was supposed to be.

Why would he be watching her?

"Thanks! This is awesome!" Dylan clutched the electronic spelling game to himself. "I've been wanting one of these forever."

"Hey, buddy, come show me your new toy," Bill said.

He hopped up and took it to Bill, who examined it thoroughly, praising it so that Dylan nearly beamed with pride.

Once all the kids had eaten cupcakes, fruit and cheese doodles, they cleaned up the mess.

"Children," Granny Bea said, "before it's time to leave, I want to gather in our circle one more time. Mr. Kennedy, while we gather, could you please make copies of the worksheet I left on Lindsay's desk?"

He saluted as he went to do her bidding. Poor Granny Bea.

Obviously, she hadn't told him yet the news she was going to tell the students.

The kids collected their book bags and sat on their carpet squares in a circle on the floor.

Granny Bea put her finger over her lips to hush a threesome that was chattering. "Listen up. I need to tell you something." Once everyone quieted, she said, "I wanted to tell you that I'm going to be moving."

Their little faces registered surprise. "Is it far away?" asked Dylan.

"I'm afraid it's too far for me to keep working here. But the good news is that I get to live with my grandson, Bill!"

Dylan stared at his feet.

"It'll be okay. Your friends will still be here," Lindsay said, trying to reassure him that some things would stay the same.

"So you'll be here, Miss Lindsay?"

"Of course I will." Yes, trusty old Lindsay would be there while Granny Bea and Bill would be one thousand miles away. She fought the frown that tried to form from merely considering that thought.

Dylan wrapped his arms around her waist. "I'm glad."

Once Dylan let her loose and picked up his book bag, she turned toward Bill. He glanced away, but not quickly enough. He had been watching her.

As the younger children were leaving, Bill's cell phone rang. "Hello?"

"Hi, Bill. Vinny, here. I've got everything ready for the house and will be going by this afternoon to place a For Sale sign in the yard."

"Great. Thanks for getting on it so quickly."

"Oh, and Donna Rae wanted me to invite you to dinner tomorrow night. About six-thirty if that would work for you."

"Well, I'm not sure, Vinny. I appreciate the offer, but Granny and I are so busy with packing."

"She's invited, too. It'll save you from having to cook."

"Thanks. I'll check with her and let you know."

They hung up.

Good. Everything was moving in the right direction. They could pack up the majority of what Granny wanted to take with her, then could leave some furniture in the house for showing it.

"Granny," he called.

She walked out of the office. "Yes?"

"I'm leaving to find Internet access to contact the lab. Then I'll go home to continue packing."

"I don't think Lindsay can spare me this afternoon, dear."

"I know. I can work on the dining room and living room by myself. If I'm unsure about anything, I won't pack it."

"Pack?" Mr. Kennedy asked as he came out of the office, worksheets in hand. "Do you still have the crazy notion to head up north?"

"I thought you told him," he said to Granny.

"I tried."

"I'm afraid it's a sure thing now, Mr. Kennedy," Bill said. "The moving van comes Friday."

"*This* Friday?" He tugged on his bow tie, and his face reddened. "Not if I can help it." He walked away mumbling something to himself.

Granny had tears in her eyes as she watched him.

"I'm sorry, Granny. I know it's hard on both of you."

"Yes, it is. He doesn't need to lose someone else he lo— cares for."

So had Mr. K used the word *love?*

"I'm going to go check on him," she said.

"Oh, Granny, before I forget. Donna Rae and Vinny invited us to dinner tomorrow night."

"Okay. That's fine." She seemed distracted as she followed Mr. Kennedy into the office.

By the time Bill returned a while later, all the children had left, and she appeared calmer.

"Is Mr. Kennedy all right?"

"He'll be okay. He wants to take me out to dinner tomorrow evening, so you go ahead to Donna Rae and Vinny's."

"I'm sorry."

"I know you truly want what's best, and that you need to hurry back to work. I'll try not to make the move any more difficult than it has to be."

He pulled her to him for a hug. "I love you for taking care of me all my life. Now it's my turn to take care of you." He breathed in the smell of her perfume, thankful he wouldn't have to leave her behind in Georgia this time. "I've been so lonely for family, Granny. Thank you for going with me."

Thank You, God, for providing for me and Drake through Granny.

That evening, Lindsay took Granny Bea home after work.

As she pulled into the driveway, Granny Bea groaned. "Oh, look."

A For Sale sign. Front and center. "Oh, Granny Bea, I'm sorry."

"It was inevitable, but I hate to see it. Makes me sick to my stomach."

"There's no reason the sign can't wait until you move."

"I guess Bill would like to know everything's in order before we leave."

Lindsay's temper smoldered.

If she could do nothing else to stop them from leaving, the least she could do was try to ease Granny Bea's pain.

She turned off her car, and they walked inside. "Wow." She stood in the middle of the living room and couldn't believe the stacks of boxes all around her.

"Bill's been busy." Granny Bea hollered toward the kitchen, "Where are you, son?"

"In here." He was in the dining room, leaning over, wrapping a china bowl in Bubble Wrap material.

"We're home," Granny Bea said. "And you've made a lot of progress."

"I sure have, Granny. I hired the boy who bought your car for his neighbor to come help pack books and nonbreakables."

Lindsay's face burned. Had Bill figured it out?

Bill speared her with a look, and maybe a smirk? "I asked about Miss Jay, who it turns out is Miss J., the initial, not Miss *J-A-Y.* I was curious when she might come pick up the car. In our discussion, I learned she may live close to where you live, Lindsay. Do you perhaps know her?"

Granny Bea coughed. "I'll go start dinner."

What could she say? He obviously knew. Or heavily suspected. "I'm sure I do," she said before turning to leave the room.

"Miss J. is a very kind, generous woman," he said so softly she almost missed it.

She paused, then looked over her shoulder at him. The look on his face nearly made her weak in the knees.

He looked at her with what appeared to be longing.

The trouble was, she'd started to feel that longing, too. She imagined if he had any clue, he might see it on her face, as well.

She turned her head and went on to the kitchen without acknowledging his comment.

Granny Bea grabbed her arm as she walked in. "Did you tell him?" She chuckled.

"No. But I guess he's figured it out."

"Was he mad?"

Mad? Anything but mad. "No." *He cares for me, and I'm starting to care for him. And we can't do anything about it.*

"He's got such a good sense of humor," Granny Bea said. "I'm sure he got a kick out of it."

"Well, let's hope so. Of course, I imagine he'll be driving your car around town with the For Sale signs again tomorrow."

Granny Bea opened the refrigerator and reached in. "Signs, signs, everywhere." She sighed. "Boxes, too."

"I've gotta go pick up the boys. I'll be here at the regular time tomorrow morning."

"Good. See you then."

As she passed the dining room, she said, "See you tomorrow, Bill."

"Can you stay for dinner?"

"No, thanks. I need to get Hunter and Chase from day care." She wanted to walk on by, but stopped so she could make sure he stayed in the dining room so he couldn't see what she was about to do.

"Well, have a good evening." He gave a jaunty salute-wave, but packing tape that had stuck to his hand grabbed his hair and yanked. "Ooh!"

She had to laugh. The man was an accident waiting to happen. "Careful. Packing can be dangerous work."

He shook his head, obviously embarrassed. "Yeah. Only for me."

"I wouldn't want to change a single thing about you." *Except maybe your mailing address,* she wanted to add, but didn't, embarrassed that she'd said anything at all. "Good night."

Why had she said that?

Because she meant it. She loved how he did silly things, sometimes geeky things. It made him fun. Lovable.

Whoa. Don't go there.

She paused on the front porch to make sure he didn't follow. Once she heard packing sounds through the screen door, she continued on her mission: To relieve Granny Bea of the pain of seeing a For Sale sign in front of the house she'd lived in for most of her life.

Lindsay backed out of the driveway, pulled in front of the house, then peeked to make sure no one was around.

Nothing stirred.

She hopped out, sprinted in front of her car, rocked and tugged until the sign came up out of the grass, remembered she needed to open the trunk, ran back to the driver's side, then popped the trunk open. She slithered around the car and quickly slid the sign into the trunk. Once she'd closed it, she hurried into the driver's seat once again and raced away.

Her heart pounded. But it wasn't like she was breaking the law or anything, so she began to giggle.

The tiny giggle ended up as hysterical laughter with her practically doubled over the steering wheel as she braked at a stop sign in town.

The next part of her mission wouldn't be so easy. She had to figure out how to get the sign into Vinny's office. She thought he stored them in the back alley, so she parked on a side street perpendicular to Main Street.

Wishing she had a thirty-gallon, black trash bag to wrap it in, she contemplated going home to get one. But the coast was clear, so she snatched the sign out of her trunk and rushed it down the little alley past small Dumpsters and garbage cans. Once behind the real estate office, she saw the bin where he kept them.

Locked.

With no time to waste, she propped the sign against the side of the bin and prayed no one stole it.

Surely people didn't steal realty signs. *Except for "borrowing" them from the lawns of saddened little old ladies.*

She began to giggle again as she rushed back toward her car.

"Lindsay?"

Vinny.

"What are you doing back here?" he asked.

She was thoroughly busted. "I was returning your property."

"What?"

"Your sign. From Granny Bea's house."

"Did they decide not to sell?"

"No. I decided to save Granny Bea the heartache. It hurt her to see it out front."

"Oh, I'm sorry. I would have waited, but Bill seemed so anxious to put it up. I'll call him and apologize for not thinking of waiting."

"No! Don't do that. I took it without letting him know."

"Oh, man, Lindsay. Give a man a break." From the look on his face, he was talking about himself, not Bill.

"I apologize. Will you promise not to tell how it got back here?"

"I won't lie if Bill asks. And I'll put the sign back up if he asks me to."

"No, don't lie, but don't volunteer the info, either. Pretty please?" She pasted a pitiful expression on her face, one she'd seen Donna Rae use before.

"I won't tell on you if you promise to come to dinner tomorrow night."

"Why on earth would you ask for that as a favor?"

"Donna Rae is trying a new recipe, and—"

"No need to say more. I'll come be a guinea pig and promise to get you out of any sticky situations where you might get yourself in trouble."

"Thanks, Lindsay. We'll call it even."

"Well, I guess I better go pick up the boys."

"Six o'clock tomorrow. Don't be late."

She waved and hurried away before he changed his mind and called Bill. Because she was getting the good end of their deal.

Her life had turned insanely crazy since Bill arrived. She'd resorted to buying cars on the sly and to relocating yard signs.

And now she'd have to go work at Granny Bea's on Tuesday, where he would try to cook her breakfast—too intimate in her book, even with Granny Bea there. And where he would be in close proximity all day long.

Unless…

She laughed at the sheer genius of her newly forming plan, which involved the Quilting Beas.

Close proximity wouldn't be a problem if she called in the troops.

Bill wouldn't know what had hit him.

Chapter Fifteen

Birds chirped outside Bill's window when he awoke Tuesday morning with a grin on his face and a hopeful spirit.

Lindsay liked him, tape in his hair and all.

Could there possibly be more? Might she learn to love him? Like he loved her?

Yes, he loved her once again. Or maybe still loved her from way back.

The big question, though, was whether she could ever care enough to uproot her life and join him in Boston.

Well, it didn't matter that he was flying out on Saturday. That he had to be back at school on Monday. He wouldn't look that far ahead. He wanted to enjoy the present. They had a whole day to spend together. No worries allowed.

He hopped out of bed and showered. Before Lindsay arrived, he hurried to the kitchen to cook breakfast. Since Lindsay had raved about his biscuits, he made a double batch. They could eat them with lunch, as well. Anything to impress her.

A little while later, the screen door slammed shut. His grin widened. "Come on in. Breakfast is almost ready."

He pulled one pan of biscuits out of the oven.

"I'd love some breakfast. Lindsay promised me food in exchange for work."

He turned and found Sandra standing in the kitchen. Without missing a beat, he said, "Good. I made plenty." He was thankful he'd doubled his recipe.

"Do I smell something good baking?" Donna Rae called from the living room. She walked in with Molly from Arnie's.

What was going on? Had Lindsay decided to throw a party? "Come in, ladies. Have a hot biscuit."

"Oh, that does sound good. And not the least bit nauseating. Just don't fry any bacon or sausage, okay?" Donna Rae put her hand over her abdomen.

"I'm sorry about my mom putting it in the newspaper," Molly said. "I can't change her to save myself."

"Don't worry about it," Donna Rae said. "No harm done."

Sandra grabbed several plates from the cupboard.

Granny walked in from her bedroom. "Well, look here, we have company this morning."

"We're here to help with the packing," Donna Rae said. "Heard the moving van is coming Friday."

"Yes, and they're flying out Saturday," Lindsay said, appearing out of thin air. The last one to arrive. At least he assumed she was the last one.

Sandra plopped a biscuit on her plate, letting it drop as it burned her fingers. She blew on her fingertips. "I'm heartbroken that she's leaving me. Best friends for over seventy years."

"And my house is for sale," Granny added. "Vinny put up a For Sale sign yesterday."

"For Sale sign?" Donna Rae said. "I didn't see one out there. Did you, Molly?"

"No, I didn't."

"What?" Bill pulled the second pan of biscuits out of the oven, turned it off, then strode to the front door.

Sure enough, the sign was gone. "What in the world?"

Then he thought of Lindsay. Arriving late.

He marched back to the kitchen and held out his hand. "Give me your keys."

"What for?"

"Hand them over, please."

She shrugged as if she didn't have a care in the world, then tossed them to him. "Am I blocking you in?"

He squinted his eyes, trying to read her. She continued to look him in the eye for a few seconds, but she seemed to be trying too hard to look innocent. Or maybe he was too suspicious.

All of a sudden, she became interested in the pan of biscuits. Uh-huh. Guilty.

He forged ahead, prepared to find the stolen sign in her trunk.

But it wasn't there. It wasn't anywhere to be found.

He walked back inside and placed her key ring back in her hand. "I'm sorry I suspected you. At least I think I am. Must have been some kids out pulling pranks."

She turned back to the jelly jar. "It's understandable given the circumstances. Hey, I guess you noticed I asked some of the Quilting Beas to come help today and promised them breakfast in return."

"The more the merrier," Granny said, even though she didn't look merry at all.

"Are you okay, Granny?" Bill asked.

"I'm fine." She waved off his concern. "I've got to push past the fear of change, that's all."

He could relate. He was having to push past the fear of being totally responsible for Granny.

But could he push past the fear of loving Lindsay?

And if he did, would three days be enough time to persuade her to come to Boston?

Did he dare try?

Frustrated that nothing had changed, and that Bill was following through on taking Granny Bea away, Lindsay banged around the bedroom as she packed the contents of Granny Bea's nightstand and dresser drawers.

It also frustrated her that she worried about falling for Bill.

Shouldn't she be able to hang out with an old friend without falling head over heels in love?

Was time spent with him so risky?

She taped the bottom of another book box and began to fill it with Granny's magazines and several devotional books.

"I've finished packing Granny Bea's summer clothes," Donna Rae said from inside the closet. "I guess Bill wants to store the winter things."

Lindsay sighed, then flopped down into Granny Bea's chair. "Probably. I don't know if he has that all figured out yet."

"What's wrong with you?"

"I don't want to do this."

"It's going to happen. You may as well quit pouting about it."

"No, I don't mean *this*." She pointed to the boxes. "I mean everything. Granny leaving. Bill leaving, too."

Donna Rae gasped. "I knew it! You're feeling something."

She looked around to make sure no one was within earshot. "I'm scared," she whispered.

"Of what?" Donna Rae whispered back.

"Of falling for him, of course."

"News flash." She cupped her hands around her mouth as if making a megaphone. "Falling for him would be a very good thing."

"Shh." She glanced around.

"Go for it, Lindsay. You've been too wrapped up in your job and family. Relax and live a little."

"I have no idea how."

"Then follow his lead. He seems to be more than interested, too."

"We only have a couple of days before the moving van shows up."

Donna Rae knelt in front of her. "Tell him how you feel."

"I don't even know how I feel. It's all so confusing."

"I'm your best friend, and I know what's good for you. Go for it."

Lindsay mashed her hand over her heart, contemplating the need for chest compressions to keep it going. "What if I do fall in love with him?"

"Then move to Boston and have a wonderful, happy life."

"You aren't serious."

"I'm dead serious. You deserve happiness, even if you have to move away from here to get it."

"But my family…"

"If you fall in love and marry, he'll be your family. You'll have to trust God to take care of your dad and Gregory's boys."

"I'm not sure I can let it all go like that, can totally give it to God."

"Sometimes giving up control is tough, Lindsay."

"Especially for me." She laughed, knowing that God had created her, but that He must get tired of her lack of faith. "You know, whatever I do, I'm taking my time and being very, very careful."

"You do that, then. But at least give it a try."

Lindsay huffed. "I need to chill out. Not to think so far ahead."

"'Atta girl. Take it one day at a time."

"'Don't borrow trouble,' as my mom used to say."

"That's right. So…how are you going to make your first move on him?"

"Oh, hush."

"You let me know how it goes."

"Sure. Of course." She rolled her eyes at her best friend.

"I'll see you tonight for dinner?"

"Yep. Sixish. Do you want me to come early and help bathe the kids and get them fed?"

"Sure. That would be great. I can't wait till you try my new recipe." She was so radiant, she nearly glowed.

Poor Donna Rae. Whenever she was pregnant, she started trying to create recipes that wouldn't upset her stomach. They were always horrible.

Lindsay would pull a pound cake out of the freezer and take it with her. Vinny and the kids would probably cry with relief.

* * *

After they finished packing for the day, Lindsay helped Granny Bea get ready for her dinner date with Mr. Kennedy at a local restaurant.

Granny Bea was radiant when Mr. Kennedy arrived, all spiffy and smelling nice. After seeing the happy couple off, Lindsay told Bill she'd see him on Wednesday, then left.

An evening with Donna Rae and Vinny was like an evening with her family. So when she stopped by her house for the cake, she didn't change. She kept on her most comfortable jeans and worn T-shirt.

Then she headed straight to their house so she could help with the kids. She didn't see how they managed four children. And now another one on the way. It wore her out to think of it.

When she arrived, she walked in the front door. "Anybody here?"

Kidlike squeals sounded upstairs. In the bath maybe?

When she walked into the kids' bathroom, she found Donna Rae had hired a babysitter. "Oh, hi. Where's Donna Rae?"

"In the kitchen, I think."

She blew kisses to the kids and escaped to the kitchen before they tried to hug her with their wet little bodies.

Donna Rae stirred something at the stove.

Lindsay set the pound cake on the counter. "Okay, how did I rate an evening with a babysitter? I came to help get them ready for bed."

"Oh, hi, Lindsay. Thanks, but I decided to make it more relaxing. I needed a break." She barely smiled, then turned back to sprinkling grated cheese on a baking dish.

"I thought you said you were making a new recipe. That looks like your standard lasagna."

She didn't smile. Didn't look at Lindsay. "I was in the mood for it. Grab a Coke can and have a seat."

She followed orders, wondering why Donna Rae was acting so strange. "Hey, where's Vinny?"

"He's showing a house. But he'll be here soon. At least he better be."

Uh-oh. "Are you two mad at each other?"

"No. I'm aggravated he's going to be late when we're having company."

"But I'm not company."

Donna Rae shrugged. "You're right. I should ease up on him."

They chatted as Lindsay tossed a salad and Donna Rae popped a loaf of Italian bread in the oven.

Donna Rae seemed to relax when they heard the sound of the garage door opening. A minute later, Vinny walked into the kitchen from the garage. "Mmm. Smells yummy." He kissed his wife's cheek, then leaned over and patted her pregnant-but-not-yet-showing belly. "Hi, little one. Daddy's home." He turned. "Oh, hi, Lindsay. I didn't see you."

"Hi, Vinny."

"So where's Bill?" he asked.

Donna Rae's mouth dropped open, then she glared at Vinny.

"What? Why are you looking at me like— Oh, man." He looked at his watch. "I guess I blew it."

Lindsay couldn't believe what was going on. Donna Rae and Vinny had tricked her big-time. "And you call yourselves my friends?" she said, only half teasing.

"Yes, and we're being your friends by doing this," Donna Rae said.

"Hey, no big deal," Vinny rubbed his palms together. "Just thought we'd get the two of you together without giving you time to fret about it. He'll be here at six-thirty."

"Quit giving details. You're going to tempt her to run," his wife scolded.

Chastised, he left the kitchen. "I'll go change," he called from the living room.

"Maybe I *can* get out of here before he arrives," Lindsay said. "Because I know you're going to embarrass me by pushing us together."

"Don't you dare leave."

"You're such a sneak."

"And you're such a chicken."

"I'm sensible."

"That's the truth. And how fun is a person who's sensible?"

The doorbell rang.

Donna Rae's shoulders relaxed. "Oh, good. He's early. You can't run away now."

"You and Vinny are staying, aren't you?"

"Of course. But if you act mean to Bill, we'll leave, and you'll have to entertain him. Now get the door."

She sighed as if the chore were odious. But it really wasn't. Why couldn't she seem to go for it like any normal woman would? What made her so afraid?

Maybe being dumped at the altar? Or maybe the fact that Bill left me so easily once before?

She trudged to the entry hall, fluffed her flat hair and smoothed her T-shirt. The one she had worn all day, including digging through Granny Bea's closets and drawers.

Probably smelled as musty as an antique store.

When she yanked the door open, there he stood. "Hi, Bill. Come in."

"Hi. I was surprised to see your car."

Apparently, Donna Rae hadn't told him, either. He seemed flustered. Then as he walked in the door, his head grazed the door frame and he jerked back in pain.

"Oh, man." He rubbed the spot.

She tried to push her hair off her face, knowing it looked awful. "I guess they intended to surprise us."

He reached up and smoothed her hair behind her left ear. "And a very nice surprise it is."

She stepped back from him, unsure of how to act. What to say. Even what to feel. "Bill, I—"

"Come and eat," Donna Rae called from the kitchen.

Vinny came trotting down the stairs and met them in the foyer. "Oh, hi, Bill. Glad you made it."

"Thanks." He glanced at Lindsay, then smiled. "Well, Donna Rae called. We shouldn't make the chef wait."

When they walked into the kitchen, Donna Rae was nowhere in sight.

"Where'd she go?" Vinny asked.

"I don't even see the food," Lindsay said.

The back door opened and Donna Rae peeked in. "Out here."

When they joined her outside on the patio, Lindsay couldn't believe all the work she'd done to make it romantic. Though it wasn't dark yet, candles flickered from all around. Tiki lamps burned around the perimeter. The scent of citronella wafted their way, aimed at keeping them from getting eaten up by mosquitoes.

She'd also set the table with china, silver and cloth napkins.

"Wow, Donna Rae. This is gorgeous. And not a paper plate in sight," Lindsay said.

Donna Rae laughed. "Nope. No plastic spoons, either. This is grown-up night."

"Who sent you flowers?" Vinny asked his wife, then pretended to be jealous.

"I'll never tell."

"It was the grocery store, Vinny. Don't get too upset." Lindsay smelled the bundle of flowers Donna Rae had placed in a vase as a centerpiece.

Bill held out a chair for Lindsay, then sat on her right. His knee bumped hers as he tried to scoot in. On the next try, he banged into the table leg and set the glassware rocking perilously. "Oops. Excuse me."

"I do the same thing all the time," Vinny said. "Especially when it involves breakables."

They laughed, and some of the tension eased.

Lindsay could do this. She could carry on a conversation with a man she cared about even though the two of them couldn't have a future together.

"How's Mrs. Wellington doing?" Vinny asked.

Bill filled him in, including Granny's objections to moving. "But she's coming around. It's hard on her, though."

"Especially that For Sale sign," Lindsay couldn't resist adding. She didn't dare look at Vinny for fear they'd give themselves away.

"Hey, that reminds me," Bill said. "Our sign disappeared."

"No problem. I'll replace it. You think your grandmother is rebelling?" He chuckled, but didn't look at Lindsay.

"I doubt it. Probably some kids goofing off. Of course, I did have my suspicions at first." He leaned down and looked right at Lindsay.

"Yeah. Well, I'm a likely suspect, I guess."

He smiled at her and wouldn't look away. She felt so drawn to him she didn't want to look away, either. Anytime he focused on her so fully like that, it did all kinds of strange things to her insides. It made her want to run, yet at the same time made her want to grab him and kiss him.

That thought gave her the strength to turn away. She took a bite of food, then said to Donna Rae, "This is delicious. And an elegant setup. I didn't know you had it in you."

"I'm trying to impress Bill."

"Well, I'm duly impressed. This is amazing," he said.

"It's amazing what I can do when I don't have diapers to change. Vinny, maybe you can start getting home a little earlier and find out." She blew him a kiss, then laughed.

Lindsay thought they were so cute together. It seemed they'd always been in love from as far back as she could remember. "You know, I remember how Granny Bea had imagined you two as a couple when you were in the youth group at church."

"She sure did," Vinny said.

"Of course, we also went to The Forever Tree." Donna Rae wiggled her eyebrows. "So we knew we'd end up married someday."

"Lindsay and I did a research project at the tree when we were young," Bill said. "We had to measure the girth of the trunk."

"I know. I heard you held hands around it while you were there," Donna Rae said.

"You heard that, huh?"

Lindsay's heart gave a lurch. Now he knew she'd been talking about him. "Well, if we did, it was in the name of science. It was the biggest tree there. We had to measure it."

"I did have a terrible crush on you then. I distinctly remember holding on to you as we measured." Bill smirked. "Who knows, maybe it took."

"Quit being silly," she said, but her heart still jogged around in her chest.

Vinny gave a hearty laugh, but Donna Rae, who believed in the stuff, had a hopeful look on her face.

"Stop it," Lindsay said to her. She pushed her plate away, unable to eat another bite at the moment.

"My wife is a hopeless romantic," Vinny said. "She can't help holding on to that old legend. But like Mrs. Wellington has said before, prayer and hard work have been what's kept us together." Vinny smiled at his wife before turning to Bill. "Tell us a little about your job up there in Boston."

"Well, I recently heard we got a grant for a big research project."

"Congratulations," Vinny said. "That's great news."

Donna Rae glanced at Lindsay. "So, how do you feel about it?"

At first Lindsay thought Donna Rae was talking to her, but then she realized she'd asked Bill the question.

"Honestly, I have mixed feelings. It's the culmination of two years of work, and I should be thrilled. But it means I have to rush Granny out of Magnolia sooner because of it."

"Yep. Giving her a whole week to adjust to the idea," Lindsay said.

He stared into her eyes. "There are reasons that I hate to leave, you know."

"We'll be right back. We need to tell the kids good-night." Donna Rae hopped up, upsetting the table a little herself. "Don't we, Vinny?"

"Uh, yeah. Of course."

Once they'd gone inside, Bill took hold of Lindsay's hand. "Although this project is something I've wanted for a long time, I don't want to leave you."

"Bill…"

He rubbed a gentle path across her knuckles with his thumb. "Let me say what I need to say."

"But it doesn't matter. What matters is that you and Granny Bea are leaving on Saturday."

"I know Boston and Magnolia are a long way apart, but I've been wondering…"

Her face, neck and ears burned. She knew where he was headed. Could see it in his eyes. Could feel it in the way he caressed her hand. *No, no, no….* "Of course we can be friends, just like old times."

He gave her a heart-melting tilt of his lips. A semismile. "I'm thinking light-years beyond that."

His slow grin sent her stomach to her toes and back. "Bill, I don't think—"

He leaned very close. "Let me see if I can word it more clearly. I want to be more than friends with you, even if it has to be long distance." He leaned even closer, heading toward a kiss. He stared at her lips until he was so close she—

"I don't do long distance," she blurted. "It's too hard on couples."

"This'll be different."

She put more space between them, because she couldn't think straight with his lips so dangerously close. "Joey was a good guy, but while he was off at college, he was falling in love with someone else. And he felt so guilty he tried to move ahead with the wedding plans. He didn't face the truth until the day of the wedding."

"Listen, Lindsay. I'm not Joey. I promise I wouldn't do that to you. I—" He leaned in close once again, as if he sensed her weakness. "I care about you too much."

"You left me once before," she whispered.

He stared into her eyes. "I had to. Because I loved you and couldn't watch you marry someone else."

The night air stilled, and his words seemed to reverberate between them.

He'd left her because he loved her?

"Auntie Lintsee, Auntie Lintsee," a little voice squealed from the back door. Donna Rae and Vinny's toddler, Ruthy, came zipping out the door in a diaper with her mom hot on her trail.

Perfect timing. Lindsay scooted her chair back from the table.

Ruthy dove into her lap. "Nite, nite." She wrapped her sweet arms around Lindsay's neck, the powdery scent of baby shampoo causing a longing stronger than ever before. It seemed having a man tell her he once loved her intensified the baby shampoo effect.

"I'm so sorry." Donna Rae was huffing and puffing, out of breath. "I couldn't catch up with her."

"It's okay." She kissed the toddler. "Nite, nite, sweetie."

"Ruthy, time for bed. Let's let Auntie Lindsay and Bill talk." She smiled a strained smile. "Sorry." She hustled her baby back inside.

Bill scooted his chair so they were knee to knee. "Now, where were we?"

"You were telling me you loved me in high school." And she'd rushed to see Bill to show him the engagement ring. "If only you'd said something then."

"If I had, then what? You would have avoided me. And I wouldn't even have had your friendship."

"But we were good friends. We could have talked about it. Who knows what might have happened?"

"Come on. Put yourself in my place. You know I couldn't stay around."

When he put it that way, he was right. What if it had been the reverse? She couldn't have watched him marry someone else. "Well, maybe so. But you could have come back once Joey jilted me."

"And watched while you met someone else to date and fall for? All while I sat in the background as your best buddy?" He shook his head. "I wanted to be there for you. But I couldn't do that to myself."

She couldn't believe that's what had been going on all along. He hadn't simply deserted her. He'd been protecting himself. "Well, at least the truth is out now."

But it didn't change matters in the present.

For all the feelings she had for him, and—after the baby-scented hug—longing for a child, she couldn't see how the two would ever go together. And if she invested herself in a long-distance relationship with him, well, she wouldn't do long-distance again, so it didn't matter. And even if she would and it didn't work out, she might never get the opportunity to meet a man near home, a man who could give her the family that she craved.

Her mind felt like a big jumble of questions and possible scenarios.

Not a basis for a relationship.

"Bill, I'm sorry, but I think you've gotten the wrong impression about my feelings. I'd like for us to simply be friends."

The confident, earnest man seemed to withdraw before her eyes. "I understand. I apologize."

She'd offended him. He withdrew further—physically and otherwise. Whether she'd wanted to or not, she'd hurt him. But what other choice did she have?

Chapter Sixteen

Bill couldn't get through the meal fast enough. Donna Rae and Vinny finally returned, but the rest of the dinner was strained.

Lindsay obviously didn't feel anything at all for him other than friendship. She refused to try to be more. How could he have let himself love her again—knowing that she would only see him as the geeky kid from middle school who'd practically slobbered over her all through high school?

He excused himself as early as he could. Before dessert, even.

"You can't go before having some of Lindsay's pound cake," Vinny said.

"I appreciate it, but I'm exhausted. And we have another big day ahead of us." He turned to Lindsay. "I think I'm going to need Granny to stay home tomorrow. Can you manage at the community center with your volunteers?"

"Sure. I can come help pack after I get off work."

"No. Thanks, though. We'll manage. You and the others gave us a big jump on it today." He stood.

Vinny stood.

"No, all of you sit. Eat your cake. I'll walk around outside to my car." He started down the back steps and waved. "Thanks again for dinner."

Once he'd climbed in the car, he leaned his head back against the seat. Closed his eyes. *Lord, was I so off base letting myself think she could love me back? Am I that hard to love?* Because if she loved him at all, it seemed she'd be willing to risk trying a relationship.

Well, if nothing else, his brother and his granny loved him. He had family. And Granny would be living with him soon.

He started the car and drove toward home.

A few minutes later, he pulled in the driveway. Mr. Kennedy's car was there.

He slipped inside, hoping to go to his room and not disturb them. But he didn't hear them or see them anywhere. Concerned, he walked through the house. Then he heard them through the screen door.

As he approached to tell them he was home, he noticed that Mr. Kennedy was down on one knee in the traditional pose of a man proposing.

Bill quickly stepped to the side of the door and plastered his back against the wall.

"I know I'm an old man, but I am younger than you." He chuckled.

Granny laughed, too.

Oh, no. How could he get out of there without being spotted?

"I love you, Bea. I don't want you to move. Please stay and be my wife."

Bill closed his eyes and wanted to cover his ears. But he couldn't bring himself to do it. Still, he was invading their privacy.

He scooted along the wall to try to get out of earshot.

"Jasper, I truly do care for you. But I can't do that to my Bill. He needs me."

Bill froze. Granny was saying no because of him?

As soon as he got to the hall doorway, he shot out of the kitchen. *Why did I have to hear that conversation?*

Poor Mr. Kennedy. It was amazing how parallel their two

lives were running at the moment. *I care for you, Bill, but only as a friend. I care for you, Jasper, but not enough to stay here.*

He sighed as he climbed the stairs to his boyhood bedroom. But there wouldn't be any comfort found there tonight.

"Okay, Lindsay. Spill it," Donna Rae said once Vinny left the kitchen.

They'd washed the dishes and put away all the romantic entrapments—candles, flowers.

So much for Donna Rae's sneaky plan.

"I don't want to talk about it."

"How can I help if you don't tell me what happened?"

"There's not a thing anyone can do. He said he cares for me and asked if we can have a long-distance relationship. As more than friends."

Donna Rae's face lit with a huge grin. "You dog! Why didn't you tell me sooner? You should be jumping-up-and-down excited."

"I went the long-distance route once. You know how that turned out."

"Oh, phooey. It turned out for the good if you ask me. You didn't love Joey. He was convenient."

"What do you mean convenient?"

"You wanted to get away from all your responsibilities. He promised to take you far away."

"That's so off base."

"Go home. Think about it. You'll see I'm right."

Lindsay shook her head. "I do love you, you know, even if you're half-crazy."

"I'm sorry about tonight."

"Hey, you were only trying to do me a favor. I appreciate the thought." She hugged her friend. "I better go."

"I have to say this, even if you don't want to hear it."

Lindsay stepped back, then sighed. "Okay. If you have to."

"Don't miss out on a good thing because you're scared."

"Better to have loved and lost and all that jazz, huh?"

"No, I think you need to widen your perception of what God has planned for your life."

"Okay. Your opinion has been duly noted."

Donna Rae shooed her toward the door. "Go. You're being hardheaded and I won't be able to change your mind. Not today, anyway."

Lindsay waved as she walked out to the garage. "Thanks for the great lasagna."

I'm scared, huh? And not open to God's will?

Like Donna Rae could know God's will for my life.

As she slowly drove home, she, being the rational person that she was, considered all Donna Rae had said.

God's plan for her life…. Hmm….

Well, first, there was her family—her dad, brothers, nephews.

Second, her job—directing the community center, and caring for Granny Bea. Well, looked like it was time to start looking for a new part-time job to fill that void.

Third, her church—including committees she'd recently retired from so she'd have more time for her life.

And fourth, there was travel—something she'd always dreamed of, but so far had been limited to trips with the seniors' group. She'd have to find a new roommate for those overnight trips now.

Lord, is this what You had in mind for my life? Sundays with my family. Helping take care of Hunter and Chase. Work. Church committee meetings. Trips with the seniors.

Not a moment too soon, she whipped her car into the driveway at home. Anguish welled up, it seemed, from the tips of her toes.

I want so much more. Oh, Lord, I want so much more.

She laid her head against the steering wheel to sob, and inadvertently honked the horn.

She cried even harder.

I want someone to love me. I want my own family. My own children.

How had she managed to ignore those needs for so many

years? Had she been so sure she'd never have them that she'd been afraid to hope?

Lord, I have to trust You with this. I can't manage it on my own. I can't control it, and I don't even want to try.

Help me. Show me what You have planned for my life. I know You planned good things for me.

She turned off her car, climbed out and went into her quiet, lonely house. The house had been her grandparents', and when she'd been little, she'd played dress-up in the attic. As she grew older, she'd played dress-up with Grandma's wedding dress. She would put it on and dream of the man she would walk down the aisle with someday.

But then Joey had destroyed those plans. He'd left her with Grandma's refurbished gown and a broken heart.

And he'd left her stuck at home caring for everyone, putting them before herself, putting them before her dreams of going away to college. He'd left her trapped in Magnolia.

Donna Rae was right.

She picked up the phone in the kitchen. When Donna Rae answered, Lindsay said, "You're right. And I apologize for doubting you."

"Oh, hon. I'm sorry. I can tell you've been crying."

She sniffed, then yanked a tissue out of the box on the counter. After a nice, loud nose-blowing, she said, "I wanted an excuse to go away, and Joey was my ticket to leave guilt-free."

"Sweetie, you always did put too much pressure on yourself to fill your mom's shoes. No one could tell you otherwise."

"But I felt as if Dad needed me. As if they all needed me."

"And they did. Even though they didn't want to, they did."

She scooted the stool from under the kitchen counter and sat. She didn't know what to say. What to do.

"You know what you've got to do now, don't you?" Donna Rae asked as if she'd read her mind.

"I'm sure you're going to tell me."

She laughed, then a baby started wailing in the background. "You've got to quit looking backward and only look to the present. Forget being dumped, forget being held back from going away to college. You know you wouldn't trade the time you've had with Hunter and Chase since their mom lit out."

"No, I wouldn't."

"So thank the good Lord for this new opportunity and move forward."

"What kind of opportunity is it to try to date someone who's a thousand miles away?"

"You know, you're going to have to figure everything out. All I can do is tell you I think you need to jump on this chance for love." The squalling escalated, and Lindsay could tell Donna Rae had picked up whoever was crying. "Gotta go. Call me tomorrow." *Click.* She'd hung up.

A chance for love.

Exactly what Lindsay had been praying for. Someone to love her.

But Bill? All the way from Boston?

Wednesday morning seemed quiet to Bill without Lindsay stopping by to see if Granny needed a ride to work.

He and Granny enjoyed a last cup of coffee on the front porch swing before jumping on the packing. She was less talkative than usual. Maybe because the For Sale sign was back and glaring at them from near the road.

A bird chirped nearby. The swing made a gentle squeak as they slowly moved back and forth.

"Granny, I have a confession to make."

"I can't imagine what."

"I came home early last night. Found you and Mr. Kennedy out back."

"Oh, dear." She gripped the hem of her blouse. "How much did you hear?"

"Enough."

"I'm sorry, Bill."

"No, I'm sorry. I tried to move away before overhearing anything, but I couldn't go fast enough."

"I don't want you to worry yourself with it, son."

"Granny, I'm so torn. I want you with me more than anything, but I don't want to stop your happiness with a man you love."

"Hush. We're not going to talk about it. You weren't supposed to even know."

"But I do know, and I don't like it."

"Life goes on, sometimes not exactly as we had planned. But it goes on anyway. Now…" She patted his hand. "What I do want to talk about is how you feel about Lindsay."

He shook his head. He didn't need her picking up on the fact he was in love. She'd never drop it. "There's nothing to talk about."

"There is. I can see it. What are your plans where she's concerned?"

"She's not interested, so there aren't any plans."

"Pish-posh. She is too interested. She won't admit it."

"How do you know?"

"Believe me, I know Lindsay. You need to help her accept the fact that you love her."

He raised his brows at Granny. "And how did you deduce the fact that I love her?"

"Grannies are all-knowing."

"Uh-huh. If you're so all-knowing, then perhaps you'd tell me what the outcome will be."

"Depends."

"On what?"

"On how convincing you can be when you take Lindsay out on a date tonight."

"Granny…"

"Of course, you can always trick her into holding hands around The Forever Tree again. Maybe that would work."

He pushed up from the swing. "Come on. Let's go to work. No more fanciful thinking."

"Okay, dear. Help your ol' granny up."

He pulled her to her feet, gave her a quick hug, then followed her inside. "I'm going to try to make headway in the attic and garage today," he said.

"Sounds fine. I'll pack the small kitchen items I'll want in Boston."

He headed up the stairs to try to sort through everything in the attic before it got too hot.

After about an hour, he came across two boxes. One marked *Bill,* the other marked *Drake.*

He opened his box and found what looked like piles of school papers and other mementos: his high school graduation program, his tassel, his college acceptance letter. Then as he dug deeper, he found older work. A research paper on Mars. A book report on a hugely thick, nonfiction book he remembered reading in middle school.

Off to the side of the older pile, he found the small book bag he'd used in middle school for science projects—something he'd done not only for school, but also for fun on his own.

He pulled it out and opened it. Three logbooks were inside. He opened the first one and smiled at how precise he'd been even then, meticulously recording whatever data he was collecting at the time.

The second book was nearly empty. He'd quit doing research for fun when he got older and homework took more of his time.

He opened the third book and realized it wasn't his handwriting. Then a jolt of awareness hit him.

It was Lindsay's handwriting. From their science project together.

Granny's words rang in his head. *Of course, you can always trick her into holding hands around The Forever Tree again.*

Another shock wave surged from his insides out to his fingers, making them almost tingle.

Could he really do it? Could he lure her back to the tree and share this journal with her? Maybe if they held hands again, she would realize she cared for him more than just as a friend.

Could the tree work its magic?

Lord, I know there's no such thing as magic. But I could sure use some of Your divine intervention right now with Lindsay. If that's what You want for our lives.

I do want Your will, Lord. Help me remember no matter what happens that You're going to be with me.

He put the logbooks back into the book bag and carried it downstairs. He dialed Lindsay's cell phone number, and it went straight to voice mail.

He hung up. Maybe he should think about it some more before asking her out. Maybe the fact she didn't answer was a message for him.

Now he had to put it in God's hands.

Lindsay's cell phone rang while she was on her way to the community center. *Gregory.* "Hey, what's up?" she answered.

"Emergency. I need a mom."

"What?"

"I need you to play mom. Tomorrow morning. Breakfast with Mom at the day-care center. The boys won't get doughnuts with the other kids unless they produce a mom or a grand-mother."

"That's terrible. Why can't they include all the kids?"

"The teachers sent a note home a while back that said it was okay to bring a female relative or friend. But the boys kept begging me to call their mom. They were so sure she would come. I couldn't risk it, so I set the note aside. Now they're having a fit, thinking they won't get doughnuts."

She could imagine their hurt at not ever having their mother be there for them. "Oh, Gregory, I'm sorry. Do you think they understand?"

"I told them she's really busy so we can't call her. Hunter cried himself to sleep last night."

A physical pain pierced her chest. "Oh, poor baby. Of course I'll do it."

As much as she wanted to claim time for her own life, she had to look at the priorities. And Hunter and Chase were priorities right now. Once they were older, or once Gregory remarried, then she could focus more on herself.

For now, helping Gregory raise the boys was more important.

Chapter Seventeen

Lindsay arrived at the center, but fretted all day about Hunter and Chase. She managed to get through the workday, but it was miserable without Granny Bea there. The woman was the sunshine in the center. Nothing would be the same.

Though Bill had refused Lindsay's help for the day's packing, she wanted to drive by Granny Bea's house on her way home. She wouldn't go in, but wanted to see if Bill's car was there. To see if they were home. They were.

And the For Sale sign was back.

Poor Granny Bea.

She looked up and down the street. No one on their porches. No cars driving by at the moment. It would only take a few seconds to swipe it one more time and return it to Vinny. Maybe he'd get the hint this time and wait two more days before replacing it.

It would be a small last favor for Granny Bea.

She pulled to the side of the road and hopped out.

Bill thought he heard a car out front and peeked out the living-room window.

Lindsay's car. Stopped on the side of the road. And Lindsay…
She was stealing the sign!

It wasn't vandals after all. It was his misguided friend.

A friend who loved his grandmother enough, who cared about her feelings enough, that she would risk taking something that didn't belong to her.

And risk frustrating him.

He laughed. It was why he'd always loved her.

And now loved her even more. She was sweet, kind, fun, devoted.

Creative.

He wouldn't stop her. But he might have to tease her about it. Later.

On their date.

Yes, he would call her back and invite her out for dinner. And he would somehow take her to The Forever Tree.

Forever…

Thoughts of spending that time with Lindsay made him smile.

He quickly pulled out his cell phone and dialed her cell phone. It started to ring from his end right as she began to drive away. Would probably give her a big scare.

Sure enough, her brake lights came on and she jerked her vehicle to a stop.

He hid so she couldn't see him in the window.

"Hello?" She sounded scared.

"Hi. I've found something in the attic that I think you'll be interested in."

"Is this Bill?"

"Of course."

"What did you find?" Her car began moving again. Rather quickly.

"You have to have dinner with me to find out."

"When?"

"Tonight. I'll pick you up in an hour." His heart began to pound because he was so sure she would refuse.

Silence. "You've got me curious."

"That's the point."

She laughed. "Can we go as just friends?"

"If friends is all you want to go as, then I suppose so."

"It's all I *can* go as."

"Then I guess I'll have to be satisfied."

"Okay. See you in an hour."

Lindsay returned Vinny's sign, then fretted for a half hour about what to wear for their dinner. Determined to quit worrying about something so insignificant, she freshened up her work "uniform"—khaki pants, a summer sweater and comfortable flats.

Of course, about ten minutes after she made that decision, Bill called to tell her to dress casually. He had a surprise for her, and they would be outside.

So back to the closet she went.

By the time Bill arrived, she had on a pair of shorts, a sleeveless top and flip-flops. Which went perfectly with his shorts and polo shirt.

He stood on her front porch, smiling.

"Hi."

"Hi." He pulled a bouquet of flowers from behind his back.

"Hey, this was supposed to be two friends going to dinner."

"Friends give flowers to friends."

"You're right. Thanks." She waited for him to give them to her, but he didn't. He stood there grinning like a fool. A wonderful fool. A giant of a man with a giant heart.

She gave him a smart-alecky look. "Do I get them or are they part of your outfit?"

"Oh! Sorry." He chuckled. "I was momentarily blown away by how spectacular you are."

As she stepped toward him, reaching for the flowers, he stepped forward, as well, and stepped on her toe. She winced, even though she tried to ignore the pain.

"Oh, I'm so sorry."

"It's okay. Let me put them in water."

She noticed one side of the bouquet was crunched. Apparently, he'd been a little rough on them. She bit her lip to keep from grinning, then held them against her so he wouldn't see it. He would feel as bad as he had over her mashed toe.

Once the flowers were arranged, they left the house. "So, where are we going?"

"I had a craving for Minnie's Meat and Three."

"Oh. Okay." She tried to hide the surprise, but didn't manage very well. It wasn't supposed to be a real date, so it wasn't such a bad choice. They would have good food.

Still, disappointment made her want to frown. But she resisted.

He chuckled. "I think you'll have fun."

They drove toward the downtown square, pulled up to the curb in front of Minnie's, but he left the car running. "Stay here. I'll be right back."

A few minutes later, he appeared with a picnic basket in hand and a jug of what looked to be iced tea. He opened the trunk, disappearing out of view for a couple of minutes.

The trunk slammed shut. Then he jogged to the driver's door. "All set."

"So we get our favorite food in a mysterious locale?"

"Yes. I hope you'll enjoy it."

"Sounds perfect. So where to now?"

"You'll see."

He whistled a tune that sounded a little like a hymn. Probably something Minnie had been whistling.

He drove three quarters of the way around the square, then pulled into a parking space behind the courthouse. "We're here."

"Eloping at the courthouse? How forward of you." She tried not to smile.

"Maybe if I were a more ambitious man. However, I just plan to make you fall in love with me tonight." He grinned at her, then hopped out of the car.

Lindsay sat frozen in place. Though he was obviously teasing, the tone of his voice, the look in his gorgeous golden-brown eyes, everything about him indicated he was totally serious. She forgot to breathe and had to practically gasp to catch up as he came around to her side.

He opened her door and held out his hand. "Come on, let's get the stuff."

She hesitated, but then placed her hand in his. It was warm. And he seemed sure of himself as he held her hand. The next thing she knew, he was letting go to open the trunk, and she missed the contact.

Inside his trunk sat the picnic basket. He also had a large canvas bag with supplies. He handed her what appeared to be one of Granny Bea's quilts—the oldest, most worn one.

"Did you get your grandmother's permission to use this?"

"She and I have used it in the yard for picnics for twenty-five years."

He grabbed the heavy items and left her with the quilt and jug of tea. As she'd presumed when they parked, they walked across the street to the city park. There weren't many people out because it was dinnertime. Plus, it was a fairly hot, muggy evening for May in Georgia. Most people in their right minds would be inside with air-conditioning.

They entered the park through the ornate ironwork archway. He led them to the back right corner.

Toward The Forever Tree.

"You're being a little obvious, Bill."

"Humor me. I have a method to my madness."

"Aha. Dinner with the mad scientist."

He took the quilt from her and spread it on the ground. "Actually, I'm doing an experiment here tonight."

"And I'm the guinea pig?"

"No, you're a scientist, too. But first, dinner. While the food's still hot."

The spread was amazing. Not only had Minnie packed a lovely dinner, but Bill had also thought of all the little details—insect repellant, a candle, his iPod player with portable speakers, and…romantic music?

"How did you get romantic music on your iPod device when you don't have Internet access at your granny's house?"

"Why would you think I had to download it recently?"

He'd left her pretty much speechless. And embarrassed. And a tiny bit jealous. Well, maybe not *jealous,* exactly.

"I wish you could see the look on your face, Lindsay."

"I realize how silly my question was."

"Not silly at all, because I stopped by Gregory's on the way to your house this evening and downloaded this playlist."

"Well, a girl, even a friend, needs to feel special on a dinner date, not like she's getting a recycled romantic ploy. So thank you for fessing up."

"You're welcome. And you're definitely special."

They enjoyed Minnie's delicious food and managed to stay cool under the shade of the huge pecan tree. As they polished off the last of the meal, she asked, "So what's this experiment you were talking about?"

He cleared the dishes. Wouldn't let her help at all. Then he pulled out an old backpack from the bottom of the large canvas bag. "Recognize this?"

"No."

He laughed. "It's my research book bag. I found it in Granny's attic while I was packing."

"Did you find anything inside?"

"Sure did." He opened the backpack and carefully pulled out a composition book. "Our science project logbook."

A hum buzzed through her body, making an audible sound in her ears. At least she thought it was audible. "I can't believe it."

He opened it almost reverently and stared at the first page. "'The Scientific Method. Step 1. The Question. How much bigger around is tree number one than tree number two if number one has plenty of sunshine and tree number two is in the shade?'" he read.

"I guess we didn't take any other variables into consideration," she said. "Like the age of the trees."

"In sixth grade? We were doing well to actually do research and then to turn it in on time."

"So what was next?"

He scooted closer to her on Granny Bea's quilt so she could see the notebook. "'Step 2. The Hypothesis. We think the tree in the sunshine will grow bigger by a lot.'"

"Ooh, very scientific amount. *A lot,*" she said. "That sounds like one of my contributions. It probably made you break out in a cold sweat."

He laughed. "No comment. 'Step 3. The Experiment.' At this point we wrote all the details about how we would come to the park and measure the trees with a measuring tape exactly four feet from the ground."

"Impressive."

He pointed to the pages. "Notice, it's in your handwriting because mine was, and is, so bad."

"What's next?"

"'Step 4. Collect and Analyze the Data.' You made a chart that showed our measurements. We measured each tree three times to make sure we hadn't done anything wrong."

"Your idea, I'm sure."

"Of course." He smiled at her. And from close range, she could see flecks of an almost red color in the brown of his eyes.

How could she have never noticed before? "So, let's see. Did the trees measure differently?" she asked.

"You don't remember?"

She looked at the results. The tree in full sun, The Forever Tree, measured four and five-eighths inches larger than the one partially under the stand of enormously tall pines. Of course, the shaded tree was no longer in the shade. The pine trees that had towered over it were now gone.

"Our conclusions say we thought the sun had made the tree grow larger than its partner," she said.

"Yes. Of course we knew nothing about determining whether or not it was a statistically significant difference."

"Hey, don't knock the research." She flipped to the inside cover of the notebook. "We got an A+."

"So, how about we do some follow-up research?" He reached into the bag and pulled out a measuring tape.

"Man, you're sneaky. I'm thinking you're just trying to get me to reach around the tree with you." She gave him a playful punch in the arm.

He smiled, yet looked solemn at the same time. Maybe it was the eyes that seemed solemn, because the mouth was smiling. "Don't need to. You've already reached around it with me."

She immediately went into another fit of panic—inwardly, of course. The exterior remained perfectly calm.

How could a silly legend that had nothing to do with reality send her into a tailspin?

Probably because she'd heard about The Forever Tree her whole life.

She popped up off the ground faster than ever before. Then she held out her hand to help him up. "Come on, let's see how much the trees have grown, and whether the shaded tree has caught up."

They first wrapped the measuring tape around the formerly shaded tree to get a reading. Then they moved to The Forever Tree.

"From the looks of it, I believe they're about the same size," she said, avoiding wrapping her arms around it.

"Are you chicken?" he asked.

She yanked the measuring tape out of his hands, then began to wrap it from her side. "I don't see how we were able to reach around this one way back then. Come grab the end of the tape, and I'll walk it around."

"Yep, you're chicken. You're afraid you'll end up falling for me and won't be able to do anything about it."

"A stupid tree can't make that happen."

"No, but God can. Plus, Donna Rae's had a feeling about us."

No! She didn't want to be reminded. She trusted Donna Rae's predictions more than an old legend. Because if Donna Rae'd had a feeling, she'd probably been praying. And if God had the two of them in some plan, well, then Lindsay was toast.

He's the one for you.

She didn't know if the thought had been her own, or if it had come from God. And she was never very good at discerning.

Well, tree or no tree, she was now officially scared to death. She may as well add a second hand-holding around The Forever Tree to the mix.

She stretched the measuring tape around her side with the end of it in her right hand. Then she felt Bill pull on the tape.

"I still don't think we can reach all the way around," she said.

"You're forgetting my wingspan."

The next thing she knew, he joined his end of the tape with her left hand and read off a number. Then, a moment later, he grasped both her hands.

She expected some electrical jolt or something. Maybe a bolt of lightning. Nothing.

But then he ran his thumbs over her thumbs. A gentle caress. She couldn't see him at all, and she wanted to. She wanted to look into his eyes and, maybe through seeing the love there, discover how she truly felt about him.

She let go of one hand, then walked around the tree still holding on with the other. The tape measure snapped closed. When she could finally see him, she noticed him take a big swallow, his Adam's apple bobbing up, then down. It was the nervous swallow of a middle schooler with a crush on her. The nervous swallow of a tall, gawky teenager with a crush on her. The nervous swallow of a handsome grown man who had declared that his lifetime crush hadn't gone away.

For some crazy reason, she wanted to cry.

Tears welled up. She blinked them away. He let go of her hand, and she missed the contact. But then he ran his thumbs under her eyes as if he knew tears might fall. She couldn't help herself. She nuzzled against his palm.

He sighed as he moved closer, then he kissed a path where his thumbs had been. As he neared her lips, he whispered, "I've loved you my whole life. And I've waited nearly that long to kiss you."

She didn't know what to do or what to say.

But then his lips met hers, and no words were necessary. Instinct took over and she kissed him back, for one brief moment letting go, indulging in hope, in dreams for the future.

No. No. No. As quick as she'd opened her heart, she slammed it shut and pulled away from him, gasping for air, for strength.

She absolutely could *not* fall in love. Because she couldn't move away to start a life with him. She couldn't leave Hunter and Chase.

"I have to go," she said before she started to weep and made a fool of herself. She tried to bolt, but his hand held tight.

"Please don't fight it, Lindsay."

"There's so much involved. It's not just you and me."

"I know you have your family and how difficult it would be to leave them. But for a moment, let's take everything else out of the equation."

It would be nice to do that for a change. To think about what *she* wanted.

He did it again—rubbed his thumb over her hand, reminding her of the connection between them.

She closed her eyes to say a prayer. *Lord, help me. Help me know what it is I want. And what You want for me.*

But no voices filled her head or made any pronouncements from heaven.

When she opened her eyes, Bill stood before her, his face so grave, so fearful.

He deserves to be loved. The same thought she'd had a while back rang through her head once again.

How could she love him from a distance? Or worse, how could she ask him to leave his job, his research grant, the possibility of his promotion, for her? "I'm sorry, Bill. I can't do this. Will you please take me home?"

"Of course." He gave her hand a small squeeze before releasing it.

They went about clearing their picnic site, then drove to her house in silence.

He saw her to the door. "I guess we'll see you before move day."

"I'll come help you and Granny Bea tomorrow after I go to the day-care center for Breakfast with Mom."

"With Hunter and Chase?"

"Yes. Gregory called in a panic this afternoon. The boys were upset that they wouldn't get to eat doughnuts with the rest of the kids."

"You're a good person, Lindsay. The best."

"No, I'm not. I'm just doing what needs to be done." *And I'm having a hard time accepting my lot in life.* "Thank you for a lovely picnic."

A sad expression made him look older. "My pleasure."

Once Bill dropped Lindsay off, he drove back by the park. How could he have botched everything? Not only was he ruining Granny's life, now he'd blown his chance to persuade Lindsay to explore her feelings for him.

Maybe he'd misread where he thought God was leading him—for Granny and for Lindsay. He had a lot more praying to do.

Well, at least they'd shared a wonderful evening despite his inadvisable plan to remeasure the tree.

He remembered, then, the fact that the two trees had measured to within about a half inch of each other. Sometime along the way, the shaded tree had caught up.

So, maybe the tree had gotten a slow start. A harsher environment had stunted it somewhat. But eventually the sun had reached it, and the tree had flourished.

Hadn't Bill done the same?

Somehow, he would bounce back once again.

Chapter Eighteen

The next morning, when Lindsay came downstairs, her dad was in the middle of her kitchen, cooking breakfast.

"Good morning. What are you doing here?"

"What does it look like?" He gave her a quick kiss, then got back to cooking.

"I appreciate it, but I've got to take the boys to Breakfast with Mom."

"Nope. You need to make Gregory stand up and raise his own boys."

"For a mom and child breakfast?"

"Yes. Exactly that. He should have told the director that his boys didn't have a mom available, so he would be going."

"And I'm to assume you told him this?"

"Yep. Early this morning."

"And Gregory's going to the breakfast?"

"Yep."

"So I don't get Krispy Kreme doughnuts?"

He laughed. "Nope. Sorry. How about oatmeal and fresh strawberries?"

"Perfect." She went to her coffeemaker and inserted a filter. "I guess, you're right about Gregory."

"Of course I am." He winked at her.

"I hope the day-care center learns something, too. I imagine there was more than one dad in that situation."

"I hope you learn something, too."

"And that is…?"

"You can't make your brother grow too dependent on you. Even if he never remarries, he needs to know he's enough for those boys."

The truth slammed into her. Dad was right. She needed to back off not only for herself, but also for Gregory and the boys. After a brief moment of elation, the fear hit double-strength.

Because now she had to make a decision about a relationship with Bill—and the possibility of going away with him.

She had no more excuses.

"Dad, do you mind if I skip the oatmeal? I think I'd like to eat breakfast with Granny Bea and Bill."

His smile deepened and his eyes twinkled. "I couldn't be more pleased."

Lindsay headed to Granny Bea's as quickly as she could. She felt…free. And amazingly younger.

Ready to try a relationship with her childhood best friend.

But it was more than that, and she had to admit it.

She'd really started to care for him.

To love him, even.

She had no idea what the future might hold, but at least she could jump right in and try loving him in whatever way the two of them could manage.

And maybe down the road…

She arrived early, before they expected her, and found Bill in the porch swing having coffee. He had one of Granny Bea's Bibles beside him and looked embarrassed as he picked it up and clutched it to his chest.

"Having your devotional time?" she asked as she crossed the porch to join him. As if it were no big deal to be caught with a Bible.

"Uh, yes." He set it on the porch floor beside him. "Have a seat."

She pointed to the book. "I'm glad you're reading it."

"Me, too. I have a lot of catching up to do."

She smiled, then started the swing with a push of her foot.

He lifted his legs so it would go. "I thought the boys' breakfast was early this morning."

"It was. But Gregory ended up going in place of a mom."

"Oh. Well, good for him."

"I'm proud of him, too. Of course, it took my dad's prodding to get him to do it. But I'm sure it'll go great." She took a deep fortifying breath. "So…I thought I'd come see if you'd make me some biscuits." She couldn't believe she was finally asking him to make her breakfast. It was a big step for her.

Instead of looking pleased, his expression sobered as he put his feet down and stopped the swing. "I'm glad you came early. I've been doing a lot of praying and thinking. And I have a huge favor to ask you."

Her heart nearly stopped. She'd never seen him look so worried. "Of course. What is it?"

"I guess you need to keep this confidential. Mr. Kennedy proposed to Granny."

"That's wonderful! I— Oh. I guess that's a problem with her moving away."

"I was up most of last night considering what to do. Granny turned him down because of me, and I can't live with that. I can't deny her this possible happiness because I want her to live with me."

Lindsay sucked air into her lungs and held it. Was he going to say he'd decided to stay in Magnolia? *Please, please, please!*

"I want to let Granny stay here. But until she marries, I wondered if you could let her live with you. A huge favor, I know. But it's the only solution I can see."

Lindsay's faced burned. Disappointment pinned her to the swing, making it hard to breathe. "She's welcome to stay with me for as long as needed. Don't worry about her at all." She truly was happy for Granny Bea.

He let out a breath as if relieved. "Thank you, Lindsay. I knew I could count on you."

"Of course you can."

"Last night, and again this morning, I felt God leading me toward this decision. It feels right. I think Granny needs to stay in Magnolia, like you said all along."

"Yes, she belongs here. Mr. Kennedy and I will take good care of her." Her voice felt wooden, stiff and formal. She tried to put a little lilt in her speech to make it more natural, but it was hard to talk with a weight on her chest.

"I think she'll cooperate," he said. "She refused to stay with you before, but with it being temporary, I think she'll change her tune."

"What about her house?"

"That's up to her and Mr. Kennedy. But I suspect, since he's in a duplex, they'll choose to live here."

"So you'll have to cancel the movers?"

Some of his relief and happiness fled as he turned serious again. "Yes. I'll cancel everything. Except my plane ticket."

Except his plane ticket.

On Saturday, the man she loved would be flying away, leaving her to care for his aging grandmother.

A task she would love to do for a woman who was like family.

But once again, she would be giving up the freedom to choose love.

Bill was surprised Lindsay wasn't jumping-up-and-down happy. She'd accomplished all she'd set out to do when she bought Granny's car and swiped the signs out of the yard. But instead of seeming relieved, she'd been quietly reserved.

"Lindsay, will you go with me to talk to Granny about her staying? She may fight me a bit, but I'm determined about this."

"Sure. Where is she?"

"Let's go find her."

While Lindsay looked through the house, Bill called the airline to cancel Granny's ticket and confirm his own flight. He knew it might be the only way to make her stay.

They finally found her out back talking to Sandra. It was good the two of them could spend their last years together.

"Hi, Miss Sandra." He waved. "Granny, could I talk to you for a minute?"

As they gathered around the kitchen table, Granny patted Lindsay's back and said, "I'm glad you're here early today, Lindsay."

"Me, too, Granny Bea."

"Granny, there's been a change of plans."

"Oh?"

"Yes. I've cancelled your flight."

Her face screwed up, highlighting her wrinkles. "What?"

"You're going to be living with me, Granny Bea. Until you and Mr. Kennedy can work out your future," Lindsay explained.

"I want you to accept his proposal, Granny," Bill said.

"But Bill, you can't mean this. I want to live with you."

"I know you do. But you have your own life to live here, and if I took you with me, I'd be acting selfishly."

"No, not selfish. You're wanting to take good care of me."

"But there are people here who love you and can take care of you. I see that now. I want you to be where you're happiest. And, if you and Mr. Kennedy choose to, to live out your life here in your home."

She shook her head. "No. You'll be lonely."

Yes, he would be lonely leaving Granny and Lindsay behind. *Lord, help me do this.* "I have all my coworkers and friends in Boston. I have a busy career. And when I checked in early this morning, I found out I may be named department head soon."

A promotion that should have sent him into orbit with excitement, but had left him cold. Still, once he got back home, surely all would go back to normal.

But what's normal now?

"Granny Bea, think about me, too," Lindsay said. "I was so discombobulated at work yesterday. The center seemed to have lost its sunshine. We need you here."

"Oh, I know you're both right. I just hate it. For you, Bill. And even for you, Lindsay."

"For me?" she asked.

"Yes, I had hoped you two would get together."

"I had, too, Granny." Bill glanced at Lindsay. "But it seems we're destined to be good friends."

Granny nodded, but still looked…sad.

He dreaded leaving. But he had to do it. For everyone involved.

Assuming Granny planned to live in her house after the wedding, he figured they could get her belongings unpacked quickly. Maybe he could head out of town a day early.

He couldn't bear the thought of hanging around, dragging out the inevitable.

"I need to talk to Jasper," Granny said. She walked out of the kitchen to go to the phone.

Bill stood, trying to look for something to occupy him while Granny made her call. "How about those biscuits?" he asked Lindsay as he pulled out the flour bowl.

"No, thanks. Let's get to work on the unpacking."

"So you think they'll decide to live here?"

"I'm sure of it."

"I don't feel much like eating anyway. I think the coffee will do." He put the bowl back. "I'll start unpacking the dining room."

"I'll take the upstairs." She lightly touched his arm. "You've made the right decision. I'm glad you prayed about it and followed God's leading."

"Yeah. Me, too."

As he walked toward the dining room, he heard Granny whisper, "Yes, I'm serious. I'll marry you." She sounded twenty years younger.

Then she giggled. "I love you, too."

Pause. Giggle. Pause. "No, sir, I'm not going to blow you a kiss."

How could something hurt and make him feel good at the same time?

Focusing on the good, he smiled as he walked into the dining room. There were tons of boxes to unpack.

That night as the unpacking wound down, Lindsay, with her tired, achy body, trudged toward the front door. "Night, everyone."

"Wait," Bill called from upstairs.

Granny Bea came to see her off, as well. "Thank you, dear. You've been a huge help today."

"I'll come back during lunchtime tomorrow. Do you want me to pick you up for work in the morning or would you rather spend the day on the house?"

"Come get me. We can work on the house at lunch and in the evening. I'm sure we'll finish tomorrow."

Bill walked in. "I've been on the phone with the airline. I'm moving my ticket up to early tomorrow morning. I think the two of you can finish easily without me."

"Bill, honey, don't hurry off like that."

Lindsay felt the same way. It was all happening too fast. "Why not stay for the weekend? You know, to let Granny Bea adjust to you leaving."

He massaged the back of his neck and gave a crooked smile. "I'm so behind that I can use the extra day in the lab to catch up."

Granny Bea tried to push the frown into a smile. "Well, you've been here two weeks. I can't ask for more."

"I really need to get back to the campus. It'll take me all weekend to get ready for the big meeting on Monday where they'll announce the grant. And maybe name the new department head."

Lindsay's chest tightened. "I'm so proud of you, Bill. I know you'll do great work on the research."

"Thanks. I suppose I'll leave it to you and Granny to pack for her stay at your house."

"Yes, we can get Gregory and Dad to help if needed."

"Thank you."

"Well, I guess this is goodbye. For now," she said.

He awkwardly hugged her, and stepped on her toe once again without noticing.

She stepped away and fought tears. "I'll see you at Christmas?"

"Oh, I'm sure I'll be down before then. Thanks to you and Granny, I won't be afraid to go to church and visit with the townspeople." He brushed her hair behind her ear. "Take care."

He stared into her eyes, and she had a split second of wondering if he was thinking of kissing her again.

"I'll leave you two alone," Granny Bea said before walking away.

He handed her a business card. "We can keep in touch by e-mail. And you have my cell phone number if you or Granny need anything."

"We'll be fine. I'm sure they'll probably want to marry quickly. No time to waste when you're eighty-three." She smiled even though she didn't want to.

"Yes, and a spry seventy-four."

Granny Bea was going to have her happily ever after. Why couldn't Lindsay?

"I'll see you soon." She forced herself to walk out the front door.

As she drove away, she saw him in her rearview mirror, waving.

Dear God, I turn him over to You. Take good care of him. And if You see fit, make him change his mind and come back. But only if he won't regret it forever or resent me.

That was such a crazy notion. He would never give up his career successes. Not even for her.

What are you willing to give up?

The words rattled around in her head, convicting her. He was giving up family to let his granny stay where she'd be happy.

What was she giving up?

That night, Lindsay tossed and turned in her bed with the feeling that something was amiss. Incomplete. As if she couldn't let the situation with Bill go.

And her brain was in a jumble. She needed to talk to someone rational.

She stared once again at the clock beside her bed, the one glaring as if mocking her.

Nearly midnight. Donna Rae would kill her.

But after five more minutes, she popped up and turned on the lamp. Then she dialed her friend's house.

Donna Rae picked up after only one ring. "Hello?"

"You sound wide awake."

"Lindsay?"

"Yes. I'm sorry. I need to talk."

She let out a heavy breath. "You scared the daylights out of me. I thought someone had died."

"He kissed me," she blurted.

She gasped. "And how was it?" Donna Rae's excitement zipped along the line.

"Very nice.... Amazing." She got lightheaded just thinking about it. "But short and sweet, since I freaked."

"Did you tell him you love him?"

"Well, no. I wasn't sure at the moment. Besides, he's leaving tomorrow."

"So, move up there with him and Bea."

"He's leaving Granny Bea here to live with me until she and Mr. Kennedy can get married."

The covers shuffled. "Whoa. When did all that happen?"

"Today."

She grunted as if moving. "So how do you feel?"

"Not as happy as I should."

"A hollow victory, huh?"

What could she say? She was thrilled and devastated at the same time?

"Do you love him?"

She huffed. "Yes. And I want him to want to move back to Magnolia."

"Lindsay, honey, you may not get everything your way. You need to pray about it."

"You're right, of course."

"Just don't be a scaredy-cat, okay?" She yawned as she finished her sentence. "And don't call me again in the middle of the night." She laughed as she hung up.

Lindsay laughed, too, as she settled back into bed. Of course, she wasn't any more clear on what she needed to do than she had been two minutes ago. But Donna Rae had confirmed she needed to be willing to give a little. And to pray.

Lord, please show me Your plan.

As she began to drift off, she imagined she saw Bill's face, moving closer to kiss her. And then she heard a voice in the distance that sounded a bit like Donna Rae's, saying, *He deserves to be loved.*

Chapter Nineteen

Lindsay awoke with a start at five o'clock the next morning. *We held hands around The Forever Tree. Twice. I can't let him go without telling him I love him. I don't have any idea what we can do about it, but he needs to know someone loves him.*

She ran a brush through her hair, brushed her teeth, then threw on some shorts and a T-shirt. She nearly tripped trying to slide her feet so fast into her flip-flops.

She peeled out of the driveway, dialing Granny Bea's phone as she went.

Granny Bea answered.

"Hey. Is Bill still there?"

"No, dear. He headed out at four-thirty this morning."

"Good grief. Was the man in a hurry to get out of here or what?"

"Why? Can't you call him?"

"No, ma'am. I need to see him. To tell him I love him."

"Oh, Lindsay, I'm so thrilled to hear it. His flight isn't until eight o'clock. Maybe you can get there in time. Go, and Jasper and I will open up the community center."

"Thanks. I love you, too, you know."

"And I love you."

They hung up. She raced to Interstate 85 and headed south toward Atlanta.

But it was after six o'clock and rush-hour traffic had already started. Thankfully, there weren't any major wrecks, just bumper-to-bumper cars inching along about ten miles per hour.

She looked at the clock at least a million times as she crept through the city an hour and a half later. Once on the south side, she sped up to a whopping forty miles per hour.

Seven-thirty. I'm never going to make it.

When she finally arrived at the airport, she prayed there would be room in the short-term parking lot.

There was. *Thank You, Lord.*

She hopped out of her car and sprinted inside.

But she didn't have a ticket, so she couldn't go through security.

She'd have to call him and hope he would come see her.

And miss his flight? Security was lined up for a mile and he couldn't make it back through quickly enough to board his flight in time.

Lord, did You make this happen? Is it better if I don't tell him now?

She checked the departure board until she found his eight o'clock flight to Boston.

It was already boarding.

She was too late.

By the time Lindsay fought northbound traffic heading back to Magnolia, then got ready for work, it was nearly lunchtime. She arrived at the center, forced herself to climb out of the car and trudged inside.

This was crazy. She couldn't drag around like a slug because Bill had left town. She had a life. She had work to do, kids to teach and care for.

"Oh, there's Miss Lindsay," Granny Bea called as she waggled her fingers toward the front door.

The woman was radiant. Happy. So in love.

And Mr. Kennedy watched her every move as if so proud of her and of himself for winning her.

Tears prickled. She sniffed them away. "Good morning, everyone. Sorry I'm late."

The children greeted her even as they prepared to leave. Once they had all been picked up, she turned to Granny Bea.

"You don't have to say it," Granny Bea said. "I can see it in your face. You're miserable."

"I got there too late because of traffic."

"I'm sure it's for the best."

"How can it be? He needs to know how I feel, and I don't want to do that by phone."

Mr. Kennedy approached, and Granny Bea held out her hand to him. They held hands like a couple of young love-birds.

"Did you miss seeing your fellow off?" he asked.

"Yes, he had already boarded by the time I got there."

"Well, sometimes love calls for drastic measures," Granny Bea said as she stared into Mr. Kennedy's eyes.

He winked at her. "Sure does."

Both of them were positively glowing with happiness. And it reminded her a little too much of what she wouldn't be having.

"Are we going to run home and do some unpacking over lunch?" Lindsay asked.

"I'm sorry, dear. We made other plans."

"Oh, well, do you want me to go do some work?"

"No, our plans include you, as well," Mr. Kennedy said. "If you'll do us the honor."

"Certainly. What is it?"

Mr. Kennedy chuckled and planted a big kiss right on Granny Bea's lips. "We're eloping. And you're our witness."

Bill stopped by the lab and his office after leaving the airport and arrived home in the late afternoon.

The house smelled stale, different, as if it belonged to someone else. And it was awfully quiet. At the moment, he wouldn't mind if Hunter and Chase made a run-through, chasing each other, squealing.

He unpacked, then checked his answering machine. Only three messages. Two from telemarketers.

One from Granny. "Welcome home, Bill," she said in a girlish, happy voice. "I hope you had a wonderful trip. Please call me as soon as you can."

Good for her. She deserved to be happy.

He dialed her home number. The phone rang until he was about to hang up.

"Kennedy residence," Granny said.

"Excuse me?"

"You've reached the Kennedy residence." She burst into laughter.

"Funny joke, Granny."

"I'm not teasing. Jasper and I eloped at lunchtime today. Went to the courthouse for the license, then over to the church to ask Pastor Eddie to perform the service."

He flopped into a chair beside the phone.

"Bill, honey, I hope you'll be happy for us. We thought it would be easier if I didn't move in with Lindsay temporarily."

He still couldn't process what she was saying. "Wow."

"Plus, we didn't want to wait. You never know when one of us might kick the bucket."

"Granny!"

"Sweetie, I hope you'll be happy for us."

"Well, of course I am. Wow."

"So, are you settled yet?"

It took him a moment to switch gears. "Uh, no. But I did stop by campus on the way home. I'll jump in full speed on Monday."

"Good luck on the promotion. We'll be praying."

"Thanks, Granny. And congratulations. I'm truly happy for you."

At least Granny could be settled, making a home with the

man she loved. She'd been blessed through the years with two wonderful husbands.

It looked as if he would spend his life with unreciprocated love for Lindsay.

And with his work. It was who he was, after all: a successful scientist. Without that, there wasn't anything left.

On Sunday, Lindsay forced herself to attend church services. She didn't want to go there and see Bill's spot empty. She didn't want to try to pretend she wasn't a little bit angry with God.

But she went anyway, plunked into the pew, and sat there stewing. *Okay, Lord, I'll go ahead and say it. How could You have let this happen? Why couldn't Bill have chosen to stay here and have what I think would be the perfect life?*

But she hadn't ever told him she loved him. How could she expect him to make that decision if he didn't know?

He was a scientist. He needed all the data to make a decision. Maybe she just needed to go on up there to deliver the news.

Her blood nearly buzzed as it picked up its pace, rushing through her body.

Why couldn't she go up there to Boston with him? Gregory was making progress with Hunter and Chase now that she was trying to stay out of the way. Granny Bea was settled and was blissfully happy, safely watched by Mr. Kennedy.

She'd been so set on having Bill make the decision to stay in Magnolia that she hadn't truly considered her other options. Especially now that she had the freedom to make her own decisions. It was time she admitted she'd used her family and Granny Bea as an excuse to ignore her loneliness, her fear.

Her dad elbowed her. Apparently, she'd been fidgeting.

She could hardly stand the waiting. During announcements about the annual fall women's retreat where Lindsay would be doing the program, she began to think of the possibilities. But then she forced herself to focus on the service. And to pray for guidance.

* * *

As soon as the service ended, she popped up and said, "I'm sorry, Dad. I have to go."

"You okay?"

Her heart nearly burst with joy. "Yes. I'm more than okay." She kissed his cheek. "I'll call you soon."

On the way out of the sanctuary, she flagged down Granny Bea. "I'm going up there. Will you and Mr. Kennedy cover the center?"

Granny Bea hugged her. "I couldn't be happier. Go. Don't worry about a thing."

Lindsay hurried home to make plans, trying to think of someone who could take over the retreat program for her. She planned to be gone by fall.

God willing and the creek don't rise, I'll be in Boston.

Chapter Twenty

B̲ill stared out the back door of his house. With all the laundry and grocery shopping done, Sunday afternoon dragged on without end. So he decided to go back to the lab.

On the way there, he passed the little church he'd visited that morning. It wasn't his Magnolia church, but the service had been nice, the people friendly. He might go back, or he might visit around some more. He would pray about it.

Once he got to the lab, he met with some students and put in a good six hours of work. By nine o'clock that night, he'd done all he could do for the day and left to go home. But sleep eluded him. He missed Lindsay. He missed Granny.

He missed that feeling of being home.

Would he ever be able to make his Boston house feel th way?

He tried to force eyes closed that didn't want to close.

Lord, lead me to the right church, and to some Christian friends. Maybe my house will feel like a home if You're in it.

It looked as if he would have to somehow find peace about the course of his life.

You've blessed me so much, Lord. I want to give You thanks in everything.

* * *

On Monday morning, Lindsay awoke in the plush Parker House Hotel, surrounded by history, so proud of herself for making the journey.

There'd been times during the previous evening when she'd been scared to death. But she'd survived her first flight.

Now, though, it was time for the biggest and riskiest journey of all.

She showered, dried her hair, put on makeup, then dressed in her best suit skirt and jacket. She slipped on pumps and changed purses. She went to the lobby of the hotel and asked for a taxi—her second taxi ride ever, the first being from the airport.

The trip was all actually very exciting. The city was gorgeous, and she couldn't wait to have Bill show her around. So awe-inspiring to think of all the nearby landmarks.

She sat back in the seat for the cab ride across the river to the campus, confident she would make it in time. She'd done some pretty amazing research work, if she did say so herself.

She had discovered the time of Bill's meeting, the building and room number. After the driver let her out, she asked the nearest student to point her in the right direction. She had to hike farther than she'd expected, yet arrived with five minutes to spare.

But then she couldn't find the room. They weren't numbered in a logical manner, it seemed. And one hallway was roped off for floor polishing.

Lord, I need You right now. Please don't let this be like the airport.

She stopped, closed her eyes, took some calming breaths.

Lord, I truly think this is Your will. Make it be Your perfect timing, as well.

"Excuse me, miss," a young man wearing a backpack said. "Are you okay?"

"Yes, I'm fine. But I'm looking for room B-212."

"I can show you if you'd like. You're in the wrong wing of the building, and it's a little tricky to find."

"Oh, thank you so much. You're a godsend."

When they reached the room, she thanked him and paused to collect herself. *Thank You, Lord, for Bill. Help me to love him.*

The small crowd that had gathered clapped for Bill at the announcement of the million-dollar grant. Uncomfortable with the applause, he held his hands up to quiet his students and colleagues. "Thank you, but I couldn't have done this without the whole list of people you see on the screen." He pressed a button on his PowerPoint presentation.

The dean came back to the microphone. "We'd also like to announce that Bill has been offered the position of department head. We feel he's more than qualified and will serve us well, should he choose to accept." He laughed. "I look forward to that acceptance as soon as possible."

Applause broke out again.

Sheepishly, Bill once again tried to quiet everyone as he looked around the room.

Lindsay stood in the back.

His heart raced to send blood to his brain as the rest of it dropped to his feet.

She smiled and gave a tiny wave with her fingers. Then she slipped into a nearby chair.

The people around him waited expectantly.

Oh, yeah. He was supposed to close up his speech.

"Thank you so much for this honor. I'll, uh…" He couldn't focus. He couldn't take his eyes off Lindsay, so beautiful in her suit and heels.

She'd be beautiful if she'd showed up in sweats.

She showed up.

For me. At least he had to assume that.

She smiled again. And he saw it. For the first time.

Love.

She loved him.

"As I said, I'm very honored. But it looks like I'm going to be moving."

"Pardon?" the dean asked. "You didn't mention that earlier today."

Lindsay shook her head. She pointed at herself, then at the floor. *Me. Here,* she mouthed.

"I'm so sorry, Dean. I didn't know until this very minute."

Apparently, those in the room had noticed him staring, because they started to look around. All eyes ended up on Lindsay.

She turned a magnificent shade of red.

"You see, I've fallen in love with a woman from Georgia and plan to ask her to marry me. I'll be relocating to be near family."

"No!" she blurted. "Take the job. We can live here, Bill. I'm here for you." Her gaze darted around the room. "Sorry for the interruption."

Her sweet southern voice soothed his soul. He'd missed it so much in the past seventy-two hours.

He left the podium and walked up the aisle toward her. He didn't stop, but grabbed her hand and led her out of the room.

Outside in the quiet, deserted hallway, he held both her hands.

She gripped his hands firmly. "I—"

"Shh. Don't say anything yet."

"But I want you to know I love you."

"You don't have to say it. I know. By your coming here. And it means more to me than you'll ever know."

"I want you to have this, Bill. Be the department head, do the research. And I want to be here with you."

"The reason I didn't accept the job offer outright was because I wanted to talk to you first—for no logical reason."

She smiled. Very flirty. "So you've been thinking about me, huh?"

"All my life I've craved family. And I've craved you. Do you really love me?"

"I really do. I tried to tell you at the airport, but you'd already boarded."

"But I can't ask you to leave your family."

"It's what I need to do—for me and for them." She reached up and touched his cheek. "I want to be with you. Period. We can make Boston our home as long as we're together."

He put his forehead to hers. Then took two deep breaths. "This is a dream come true."

"Oh, Bill. Don't make me cry."

"You're beautiful even when you cry."

"No, I'm not, and you know it."

"Well, you do get kind of blotchy and red."

She pushed away from him as she slapped at his chest. Then she laughed as tears streamed down her cheeks. "I love you, and I want to marry you as soon as possible."

He ran his fingers through her hair and grinned. "I've been dying to kiss you again."

"Well, then, Dr. Wellington, don't you think it's time?"

As his lips finally met hers and she wrapped her arms around his waist to bring them closer, he couldn't believe how truly blessed he was.

Epilogue

After spending nearly a week in Boston, with Bill acting as tour guide and companion each day, Lindsay was spoiled. But now it was time to go back to work. And she was reluctant to return home.

The beauty of the whole thing was that she would return to Boston.

Permanently.

She bit her lip to keep from grinning, something she seemed to be doing a bit too much of lately.

Nah. Can't smile too much.

She and Bill said goodbye to the city and began the journey home to share their good news.

When they arrived at her dad's house, the Sunday meal was winding down.

As soon as they walked in, Chase threw his arms around Lindsay's legs and gave her a huge hug. "Hey, there, Chase. Did you eat your peas?"

"Daddy said he'd give me a piggyback ride if I ate five." He made a face and shivered. "I twied."

She took his chubby little hand and kissed it. "Well, I'm proud of you for trying."

"Hey, what's that?" Hunter asked, pointing to her new engagement ring.

All eyes traveled to Lindsay.

Granny Bea clapped her hands together. "Praise God."

Lindsay couldn't do much but grin. And stare into the loving eyes of her fiancé.

"What? Let's see," her dad said.

She held up her hand and wiggled her ring finger, moving around the table to show it to each person.

Her brothers whistled.

"Who gave you that?" Richard asked.

"Who do you think?" she said.

"Well, you forget I've been in Atlanta and don't know what all's been going on. But I'd guess from the stupid grin on Bill's face that he may be the lucky guy."

She stretched up on tiptoe, pulled Bill by the shirt so she could reach him, and kissed him in front of everyone.

"Yes, I'm one lucky man."

"That's gross," Hunter said.

"Gwoss," Chase added.

Lindsay walked over to hug her dad. "We plan to live in Boston. I hope it's okay."

"Of course you should be up there with him. We'll be thrilled to welcome Bill to the family." He stood and started to shake Bill's hand, but ended up hugging him instead—a manly hug, including a rough slap on the back. "I couldn't be happier."

"Thank you, sir. I'm truly blessed." He looked at each and every person around the room. "I have a big family now. Something I've always wanted."

Lindsay wrapped her arms around his waist and kissed his cheek. "Yes, you and Granny Bea and Mr. Kennedy belong to us now."

"Hey, Lindsay, does this mean I can buy Grandma's house from you for my B and B?" Richard asked.

"Can't you see we're busy here?" she said.

Bill stared into her eyes. She could tell he was at peace. He was happy. And he was in love. With her.

"Bill, we need to set a wedding date."

"Yes, first things first," Granny Bea said. "We can't have you two sneaking off to elope, can we, Mr. Kennedy?"

He laughed in reply.

"I can't believe I'm going to marry the most beautiful girl in school," Bill said with a silly grin. "Who would have ever guessed it?"

"Well, we did hold hands around The Forever Tree. Twice."

"That and the good Lord doing His work," Granny Bea said.

"Amen to that," Dad said. "Now, let's have some dessert to celebrate. I made homemade ice cream."

"Woo-hoo!" Hunter squealed, Chase echoing him as they ran around the table.

Bill gently placed his hands on each side of Lindsay's face, running his thumbs under her eyes to swipe away tears.

She hadn't even realized she was crying.

"Are you okay?" he whispered.

"I've never been happier."

"And I've never been more sure of anything."

She sniffed, then laughed. "I hope so, because you can't change your mind now."

"I'm finally home," he said.

"But we won't be living here."

"Home isn't necessarily a place. Besides, you never know. We may end up back in Magnolia someday."

"Speaking of home…" Lindsay turned to Granny Bea. "I guess it's back to work tomorrow. How about I come early for coffee and to pick you up?"

"I'll throw in breakfast," Bill said.

"With your famous biscuits?"

"Anything you want."

She already had everything she'd ever wanted. And now biscuits, too.

A woman couldn't ask for more.

* * * * *

Dear Reader,

Thank you so much for spending time with me in my fictional town of Magnolia, Georgia. I've lived in towns all around the Atlanta area, and I've tried to take the characteristics I've loved best about each one to create Magnolia, a place I want you to feel as at home as I do. I hope the book has offered you a nice break from the everyday grind, a time to hang out with the folks of Magnolia and to enjoy a happy ending. Like Bill and Lindsay discovered, God truly does have plans to give us hope and a future. (Jeremiah 29:11)

I so appreciate all of you who contacted me after my first Love Inspired book, *Her Unlikely Family*. Your letters and e-mails have meant more to me than you'll ever know. I feel so blessed that God has allowed me to have a career doing something I love so much. And what a blessing you've been, as well!

I hope you let me know what you think about *His Forever Love*. Please visit my Web site, www.missytippens.com, or e-mail me at missytippens@aol.com. If you don't have Internet access, you can write to me c/o Steeple Hill Books, 233 Broadway, Suite 1001, New York, NY 10279.

QUESTIONS FOR DISCUSSION

1. In the beginning of *His Forever Love,* Bill was longing for love and family. Have you ever felt that way? Do you think loneliness would be more difficult for someone who doesn't have faith in God to fall back on? Explain.

2. Have you had to face a parent's or grandparent's loss of independence? Have you had to face that loss or any debilitating illness yourself? If so, would you share any words of advice for others going through the same thing?

3. As a child, Bill was mistreated because he was different. Has that ever happened to you? Have you ever felt excluded, even from a church group? What can you do to help include others in your groups?

4. Lindsay was afraid to love because she'd been jilted by a fiancé. Has any event in your life made you afraid to trust? How did you overcome that fear?

5. Lindsay filled her life with busyness. Have you done that in your life? Do you overextend yourself sometimes? Why is it hard to say no when it's for a good cause?

6. What can we do to make time for God in our busy lives?

7. Lindsay has always had a dream to travel, but hasn't gone far beyond the borders of her home state. Do you have a dream that is still unfulfilled? Is there anything you could do now to pursue that dream?

8. Before Granny Bea worked at the community center, she worked as a volunteer helping children. What things do

you do for others? If you don't do anything right now, what might you do in the future?

9. In the beginning of the story, Bill felt as though God didn't care about him. Have you ever been in that place? Are you still there? How might you open yourself to God's love once again?

10. Granny Bea can't bear to see the For Sale sign in front of her house. Talk about a time you've had to give up something you love.

11. Lindsay tried to ignore her longing for a husband and children. How can someone learn to be content while single? Do you think God wants some people to remain single?

12. Lindsay's brother, Gregory, is overwhelmed by raising two boys alone. Do you know a single parent who is struggling? What can you or others do to help?

13. Lindsay's good friend Donna Rae is someone who has the gift of praying for others. Do you have someone you can always call on to pray for you? If you don't have anyone, can you think of someone you could ask? Is there someone you could pray for right now?

14. Lindsay chose to take a risk and to love Bill. What makes love so risky? How can God empower us to love others?

15. Lindsay and Bill both have to heal from past hurts. Is there anything that you still deal with from your past? What are some steps you can take right now to move toward healing?

REQUEST YOUR FREE BOOKS!

2 FREE INSPIRATIONAL NOVELS
PLUS 2
FREE
MYSTERY GIFTS

Love Inspired.

YES! Please send me 2 FREE Love Inspired® novels and my 2 FREE mystery gifts (gifts are worth about $10). After receiving them, if I don't wish to receive any more books, I can return the shipping statement marked "cancel". If I don't cancel, I will receive 4 brand-new novels every month and be billed just $4.24 per book in the U.S. or $4.74 per book in Canada. That's a savings of over 20% off the cover price. It's quite a bargain! Shipping and handling is just 50¢ per book.* I understand that accepting the 2 free books and gifts places me under no obligation to buy anything. I can always return a shipment and cancel at any time. Even if I never buy another book, the two free books and gifts are mine to keep forever.

113 IDN EYK2 313 IDN EYLE

Name	(PLEASE PRINT)	
Address		Apt. #
City	State/Prov.	Zip/Postal Code

Signature (if under 18, a parent or guardian must sign)

Mail to Steeple Hill Reader Service:
IN U.S.A.: P.O. Box 1867, Buffalo, NY 14240-1867
IN CANADA: P.O. Box 609, Fort Erie, Ontario L2A 5X3

Not valid to current subscribers of Love Inspired books.

Want to try two free books from another series?
Call 1-800-873-8635 or visit www.morefreebooks.com

LIREG09

Love Inspired

TITLES AVAILABLE NEXT MONTH
Available June 30, 2009

SECOND CHANCE FAMILY by Margaret Daley
Fostered by Love

Whitney Maxwell is about to get a lesson in trust—and family—from an unexpected source: her student Jason. As she and his single dad, Dr. Shane McCoy, try to help Jason deal with his autism, she realizes her dream of a forever family is right in front of her.

HEALING THE BOSS'S HEART by Valerie Hansen
After the Storm

When a tornado strikes her small Kansas town, single mom Maya Logan sees an unexpected side of her boss. Greg Garrison's tender care for her family and an orphaned boy make her wonder if he's hiding a family man beneath his gruff exterior.

LONE STAR CINDERELLA by Debra Clopton

The town matchmakers have cowboy Seth Turner in mind for history teacher Melody Chandler, but all he seems to want to do is stop her from researching his family history. Seth's afraid of what she'll find, especially when he realizes it's a place in his heart.

BLUEGRASS BLESSINGS by Allie Pleiter
Kentucky Corners

Cameron Rollings may be a jaded city boy, but God led him to Kentucky for a reason, and baker Dinah Hopkins plans to help him count his bluegrass blessings.

HOMETOWN COURTSHIP by Diann Hunt

Brad Sharp fully expects his latest community service volunteer, Callie Easton, to slack off on their Make-a-Home project. But her golden heart and willingness to work makes Brad take a second look, one that could last forever.

RETURN TO LOVE by Betsy St. Amant

Penguin keeper Gracie Broussard needs to find a new home for her beloved birds. If only Carter Alexander, the man who broke her heart years ago, wasn't the only one who could help. Carter promises that he's changed, and he's determined to show Gracie that love is a place you can always return to.

LICNMBPA0609